MIR MOSHARRAF HOSSAIN

Ocean OF Melancholy

The Tragedy that was Karbala

T0148705

Translated from the Bengali original
Bishad Sindhu by ALO SHOME

THORNBIRD

NIYOGI
BOOKS

Published by
NIYOGI BOOKS
Block D, Building No. 77,
Okhla Industrial Area, Phase-I,
New Delhi-110 020, INDIA
Tel: 91-11-26816301, 26818960
Email: niyogibooks@gmail.com
Website: www.niyogibooksindia.com

Text © Alo Shome

Editor: Sukanya Sur
Design: Shashi Bhushan Prasad
Cover: Misha Oberoi

ISBN: 978-93-86906-50-2
Publication: 2018

Printed at: Niyogi Offset Pvt. Ltd., New Delhi, India

This book is a gift for
Sri Samir Kumar Shome
on his eightieth year

I learnt from Hussain how to attain victory while being oppressed.

—M.K. Gandhi

Contents

A Short Biography of Mir Mosharraf Hossain

Mir Mosharraf Hossain was born in 1847 to the zamindar of Padamdi, Mir Muazzam Hossain. He was the eldest son of the zamindar's second wife, Daulatunnisa. Though he was born in Lahinipada in Kumarkhali, the village of his maternal grandfather Munshi Zinatullah under Kustia District, now in Bangladesh, most of his growing-up years were spent in the zamindar's mansion of Padamdi in Rajbari District.

A bright boy from his early childhood, Mir started his education at home under a good maulvi. Later, he was admitted to Krishnanagar Collegiate School where he studied up to class five. As he was a diligent student, his father wanted him to take his education in the city of Calcutta (now Kolkata). In Calcutta, he was enrolled in Kalighat School. Unfortunately, Mir had to discontinue his formal studies before even reaching a graduate level in college, as he was needed at home to look after his family's landholdings and other properties.

The province that formed the Mir family's estate was donated in 1607 by Emperor Jahangir to the religious preacher Syed Shah Pahlowan, an immigrant from Iraq, in recognition of his good work to society. This ancestor of Mir Mosharraf was a large-hearted saint, believed to be a descendent of Prophet Muhammad himself. Besides Pahlowan, several other members of Mir's family had become missionaries too. Though they were Muslims, their just and kind attitude had won them great popularity among the followers of other faiths. The family had received the title of Mir (wise leader) from Emperor Shah Jahan for efficiently commanding the Mughal artillery. The descendants of the family preferred to use both the titles—Syed and Mir—with their names.

It is likely that Mir Mosharraf Hossain had inherited his generosity and large-heartedness from his forefathers, for he was sympathetic to the downtrodden throughout his life.

Even though Mir could not acquire a college degree, he was good at languages since his schooldays. He was deeply interested in Arabic, Persian, and Bengali literature and spent hours reading books in these scripts. Even as a student, Mir contributed his writings to various journals, mainly in *Sangbad Hitokar* (launched in 1831), edited by Ishwar Gupta, and *Gram Barta Prakashika* (launched in 1863), edited by Kangal Harinath Mazumdar. For a period of time, Mir edited the magazines *Azizannehar* (launched in 1874) and *Hitokori* (launched in 1890). Kangal Harinath Majumdar, a close friend of Mir, introduced him to the Baul singer Lalon Fakir's philosophy. Thereafter, Mir became an ardent admirer of Lalon.

Lalon's songs give expression to the purity of human spirit and are traditionally connected to a time when Bengal was inhabited by tribal people who knew nothing about sophisticated religions like Hinduism, Buddhism, and Islam. When Lalon came to know about the existence of such established faiths, he had equal respect for each of them. It is not difficult to decipher that Mir's body of writing is influenced by such high ideals. In the movie *Moner Manush* (2010) on Lalon Fakir, directed by Gautam Ghosh, the role of Mir Mosharraf Hossain was played by Anirban Guha. The movie was a joint venture of Bangladesh and India.

Mir was married to Aziz-un-Nessa in 1865. The marriage was forced upon him by people with vested interest in it, which made it an unhappy marriage. He took his second wife Bibi Kulsum in 1874 when she was only twelve years old. This was an entirely fulfilling love marriage. They had eleven children. After Kulsum's death, Mir wrote *Bibi Kulsum* (1810), a fine biographical work honouring his beloved's memory.

Mir has authored thirty-five books of which *Bishad Sindhu* (1885–1891) is applauded as his best. Of the two plays he wrote—*Basanta Kumari* (1873) and *Jamidar Darpan* (1873)— the latter is famous not only for its literary merit, but also for it being written by Mir, who, being the son of a zamindar, explored the hard-heartedness of zamindars. Similarly, his long essay *Gojibon* (1889) is remarkable because, a Muslim himself, he defends the Hindu practice of protecting the cows.

Apart from novels and plays, Mir wrote poetry, satire, textbooks, autobiography, and biography. Some of his works besides the ones already mentioned are: *Gauri-Setu* (1873), *Er Upay Ki* (1875), *Songit Lahari* (1887), *Behula Gitabhinoy* (1889), *Udasin Pothiker Moner Kotha* (1890), *Tahmina* (1897), *Tala Obhinoy* (1897), *Niyati Ki Abanati* (1889), *Gazi Miyar Bastani* (1899),

Maulood Sharif (1903), *Musalmander Bangala Shiksha* (in two parts: 1903 and 1908), *Bibi Khodejar Bibaho* (1905), *Hazrat Umorer Dhormojiban Labh* (1905), *Madinar Gaurab* (1906), *Bajimat* (1908), and *Amar Jibani* (1908–1910).

In much of his writing, Mir depicts the follies and vices of the contemporary society. In *Gazi Miyar Bastani*, for example, he criticizes the chaos and corruption of nineteenth-century Bengal in a witty style.

In addition to being an eminent writer and journalist, Mir was an able real estate manager and made his living by both the professions. He was engaged as a manager in several estates, of which his stint in the Delduar Estate from 1884 to 1892 with his beloved Kulsum, Mir states, was the happiest. He lived in Calcutta from 1903 to 1909.

Mir died in 1911, two years after Kulsum's death, and was buried in Padamdi.

The people of Bangladesh have paid respect to the memory of Mir Mosharraf Hossain by naming schools, auditoriums, libraries, roads, and a bridge on River Gorai after him.

Translator's Introduction

The novel *Bishad Sindhu*, by Mir Mosharraf Hossain (1847–1911), is an acknowledged classic in Bengali literature. Based on the history of the battle of Karbala, where Imam Hussein was killed, it is a narrative full of pathos.

After its publication in 1885, it had found immense popularity in Bengal equally among the Hindus and the Muslims. Within a year of its release, the book had to be reprinted five times. Even though Mir has other works to his credit, *Bishad Sindhu* has given him immortality. In Bangladesh, there are libraries, roads, schools, and auditoriums named after Mir. Stage shows based on *Bishad Sindhu* are often conducted there, and Mir's birth anniversaries are celebrated with honour.

As we all know, an incident that took place in Karbala in 680 CE is remembered as Muharram and is commemorated every year through passion plays, especially by the Shia community of Muslims. The heartbreaking story has also been told and retold many times by many authors in their various ways. That Mir Mosharraf Hossain, too, chose to create a novel based on the subject of Muharram is not remarkable. What is remarkable in his storytelling, however, is that along with his profound sadness for the two great brothers, he also empathizes, in a large measure, with the party opposing them.

Hassan and Hussein, the grandsons of Prophet Muhammad, were the chosen ones of their community. They were looked up to by many as their natural leaders. This dynastic approach to succession to important posts was out of tune with the 19th-century spirit of Bengali Renaissance. Mir, too, was a Renaissance man. Perhaps, that is the reason why his love for the two noble brothers is not blind. Indeed, on the basis of Mir's treatment of Yazid, the staunch enemy of Hassan and Hussein, some critics have even said that Yazid is the real hero of *Bishad Sindhu* just like the anti-heroes Ravana and Meghnad in Michael Madhusudan Dutt's *Meghnadbadh Kavya* or Satan in Milton's *Paradise Lost*. No doubt, Yazid is described in *Bishad Sindhu* as a wicked man, but he is also endowed by Mir with a glorious human quality—the ability to admire and love another human being; in this case, a gentle lady. The pain of Yazid's thwarted love is delicately brought out in 'The Story of Muharram', Part I, of *Bishad Sindhu*.

In his novel, Mir bestows the two rival parties with two opposing sets of faults. Yazid and his associates are cruel unbelievers, while Hassan and Hussein have overwhelming faith in premonitions and supernatural powers for protecting them and their people from harm. This unrealistic attitude can be reckoned as a 'tragic flaw' in the two great characters, earning for Mir's work an aura of ancient Greek drama.

A fascinating aspect of *Bishad Sindhu* is Mir's unique use of language. In fact, Mir's style of expression and the vocabulary he uses are so ingenious that they make an interesting study when related to the development of Bengali language itself. A concise account of this issue has been featured here after my general introduction to *Bishad Sindhu*.

After *Bishad Sindhu*'s publication, the book's brisk sale inspired Mir to extend the novel in two additional segments called 'Uddhar Parva' (Operation Rescue), published in 1887, and 'Yazid Badh Parva' (The Slaying of Yazid), published in 1891. Later, the three separate parts were printed together where Part I, now named 'The Story of Muharram', had 204 pages, 'Operation Rescue' (Part II) had 191 pages, and 'The Slaying of Yazid' (Part III) had only 43 pages.

It should be noted that even though *Bishad Sindhu* is a brilliant piece of literary work, it is not totally without faults. Besides being historically inaccurate on many accounts, several critics including Kazi Abdul Wadud (1894–1970) have found it carrying too many unnecessary subplots, surplus characters, and several uncalled for verbose narrative passages.

A reader may discover, though, that very few of these faults exist in 'The Story of Muharram', Part I, of the three-part work that *Bishad Sindhu* is since 1891. Mir's genius as a novelist shines through the brightest in the first part of his book (that is, in the original version of *Bishad Sindhu*). The other two parts mostly consist of lengthy descriptions of warfare.

In the present translated volume, I offer my readers a detailed rendering of *Bishad Sindhu*'s Part I: 'The Story of Muharram' and the first three chapters of 'Operation Rescue' to celebrate with Mir the symbols of Apollonian positives (that is, victory of good over evil). The rest of the few concluding pages have been done in summary.

The Language
of *Bishad Sindhu*

An attractive feature of *Bishad Sindhu* is Mir's unique use of language. He employs a highly Sanskritized Bengali to tell a splendid story of the Middle East. The novel's popularity proves that his experiment was successful.

However, the success of Mir's novel written in Sanskritized Bengali should not give us to believe that our command of Bengali is good only when it is Sanskritized. In fact, Sanskrit came to the region that we now know as 'Bengal' later than it had in many other parts of India. The territory that now comprises Bangladesh and the Indian state of West Bengal had been inhabited for centuries by non-Aryan tribes, the ancestors of Kol, Bhil, Santhal, and others, who spoke an Austro-Asiatic language and a form of inferior Prakrit (distorted Sanskrit) when people of the region came into occasional contact with the Aryans and imitated their speech. Pali, which was initially a variety of Prakrit, but had gained the status of a language through its copious use by the Buddhists, also became a popular language of the inhabitants when the region was under dynasties that had embraced Buddhism.

The Palas (750–1174 CE) were the last Buddhist rulers of Bengal. The Senas who defeated them and reigned over the region for about a century were staunch Hindus, though promoting the interests of the elite Brahmins and Kshatriyas at the cost of the common and poor citizens of other castes and religions in their kingdom. They only favoured authors who wrote in Sanskrit. The true vernacular of the region remained neglected until a representative of Sultan Qutb-ud-din Aibak (1150–1210) of Delhi, Bakhtiyar Khilji (died 1206), invaded and occupied the region, as the story goes, with only seventeen horsemen. The local vernacular received the status of a distinct language and developed rapidly only after this episode, that is, under the rule of the Sultans. (See *History of Bengali Language and Literature* by Dinesh Chandra Sen, published by The University of Calcutta in 1911, Chapter I, page 10, under the subheading 'Bengali Favoured by Moslem Chiefs'.) Even our province, a cluster of several *janapada*s, was unified by the Muslim leader Iliyas Shah (reigned 1342–1358) and given the name Vanga (which, earlier, was the name of only one of the *janapada*s in the group), the British version of which became Bengal.

The Sultans favoured and promoted the local language, as they wanted to rule over their subjects in a friendly way, making them willing participants in an all-round development of the province. The generally peaceful and willing conversion of many Hindus of Bengal to Islam during the Sultanate period, especially under the independent sultans of Bengal (1338–1538), brought about in the two communities a genuine curiosity for each other's lives and a spirit of sharing.

As a result, many Sanskrit as well as Arabic and Persian works were translated into Bengali. Several Muslim poets, including the great Syed Alaol (1607–1673), wrote in Bengali about popular Hindu personalities. Many Bengali Hindu writers had Muslim aristocrats as their patrons. Bankim Chandra Chattopadhyay in his essay titled 'Banglar Itihas' (The History of Bengal) writes,

> Under the rule of the Pathans, Bengal had brightened intellectually. Vidyapati and Chandidas, the two great poets of Bengal, had flourished during this period. The foremost original thinker of Nyaya philosophy Raghunath Shiromoni also belonged to this time. This period had, in addition, found great Vaishnava poets writing their verses. Such glorious development of Bengali literature had never happened before or since…The Pathans were our friends.

Many Persian, Arabic, and Turkic words effortlessly entered Bengali language at this time.

Peaceful coexistence of Muslims and Hindus of Bengal continued throughout the medieval period and extended beyond the mid-18th century. But complex economic and social factors strained that unity. For example, Murshid Quli Khan (1660–1727), founder of the Nawabi regime in Bengal, selectively appointed Hindus as his well-paid tax collectors; the Khilafat movement (1919–1924), in its effort to unify Muslims all over the world, discouraged a Bengali Muslim's sharing in cultural aspirations with a Bengali Hindu, and the British government's obvious attempt at polarizing the two communities, tried to break their bond.

Anyway, Sanskrit abruptly gained favour with the authors of Bengal again (that is, after the Sena rule) in the 19th century. Their fondness for it came about as a response to the praise it received from the British people. The British, who were established in Bengal soon after their arrival in India, were impressed with Sanskrit—its rich vocabulary and immaculate grammar. Flattered, many Bengali pandits promptly began to promote a Sanskrit-inspired vernacular. But our British masters loved to divide and rule, too. And, by promoting Sanskrit or Sanskritized vernaculars on the one hand and Urdu on the other, they had also tried to suggest to the Indian scholars that Urdu belonged to the Muslims and Sanskrit belonged to the Hindus of India.

It is true, nevertheless, that Sanskrit is a storehouse of Aryanized India's idioms and references from their scriptures and other literary sources. So, to master a high standard of Sanskrit or a Sanskritized vernacular, one has to have a good knowledge of the ethos of the ancient Aryan settlers of India. Mir Mosharraf Hossain excels in this matter. His awareness of the ancient Indian cosmology is extremely keen. Very often in his writings, he uses phrases like Vana Devi and Sandhya Devi. He uses such expressions confidently, knowing that in their true and original sense, they do not represent strange Hindu goddesses, but stand for attributes of natural phenomena (see my translation of Bankim Chandra's essays *Many Threads of Hinduism*, published by HarperCollins, page 13). Mir always uses the word *Ishwara* for Allah, and the phrase *upasana griha* for masjid, as their corresponding meanings are the same. But when he uses the word *atma*, which means soul, he is mindful that the Islamic and Hindu conception of its development differ.

After its publication, *Bishad Sindhu* received popular as well as critical acclaim. *Bharati*, the renowned magazine published by the sophisticated family of the Tagores, said in its springtime issue of 1886, 'The novel (*Bishad Sindhu*) is outstanding not only for its clear and exquisite language and vivid description of events but also for its fine depiction of characters...' In 1885, the summer issue of *Gram Barta* held,

> By writing several books in excellent Bengali and by editing *Ajijan Nahar* before its closing down, the novelist has already made a name in literary circles. His style of writing does not need to be praised anew. The famous story of Muharram fills the novel and illustrates the aptness of its name, *Bishad Sindhu* (*Ocean of Melancholy*). Some passages of the book are so deeply filled with pathos that a reader can hardly hold his tears.

Bankim Chandra Chattopadhyay was hugely impressed by Mir's command of Bengali. However, he applauds Mir thus, 'This Muslim scholar has written his work in pure Bengali without any trace of "Musalmani" words. His Bengali is purer than that of many Hindu writers.' (In this case, Bankim was praising Mir's play *Jamidar Darpan*).

It is startling to find how a person as rational as Bankim could use the word 'pure' as a synonym for 'Sanskritized'. But the truth is that, though genuinely charmed by Mir's style of writing, Bankim Chandra did not favour any particular brand of language. Clarity of expression was what he really appreciated. In his essay 'Bangla Bhasha' (Bengali Language), Bankim emphatically expresses this opinion of his. Towards the end of the essay, he says, 'Use any language to make yourself articulate—English, Persian, Arabic, Sanskrit, rural or wild.' We notice that Bankim emphasizes the importance of Persian and Arabic by naming them second and third after English in his list of tongues. Furthermore, Bankim had often regretted that Bengali society was fragmented (in his time) not only into Muslim and Hindu communities, but also into the upper and lower classes of society and into the educated and the uneducated citizens. It is possible that he approved *Bishad Sindhu*'s Sanskritized Bengali, finding that its author had not fallen into the trap that our English masters were using to polarize Bengali society into Muslim and Hindu compartments.

Be it as it may, Mir's use of Sanskritized Bengali for narrating an Islamic story can best be explained, I suppose, as a natural choice of one who was at ease with both the communities. There is no doubt that the author of *Bishad Sindhu* was a devout Muslim. Simply, a list of the titles of some of his other works can make the point clear: *Eslamer Joy* (The Victory of Islam), *Moslem-Birotta* (Valour of the Muslims), *Modinar Gaurab* (Pride of Medina), and others. And yet, he has also written his famous sixty-six-page-long book *Gojibon* (The

Life of a Cow) to save, with his Hindu friends, the cows from being slaughtered.

Ultimately, a creative work has to shine for its own worth, irrespective of its author's religious, ethnic, or any other credentials. *Bishad Sindhu* is a classic literary composition not because its creator is a Bengali or a Muslim, but because its universal appeal is big.

The Indian Connection

As reflected in the story of Azar, the idol worshipper in Chapter II, Part II of *Bishad Sindhu*, Prophet Muhammad and his family members were loved and respected by many non-Muslims of their time. History records the names of several Christians, Jews, and Hindus who supported Imam Hussein against his enemy Yazid, the tyrant.

During the battle of Karbala, which took place in 680 CE, many Indians, some of them Hindus, were living in Arabia for generations. It is said that these Indians were the progenies of Ashwathama—who had come and settled there—a disillusioned man, detesting his own country after his father Dronacharya was unfairly (as Ashwathama thought) killed by the Pandavas in the war of Kurukshetra.

Rahab Dutt, a Hindu Brahmin trader and an admirer of Prophet Muhammad, was a close associate of his family. He fought for Imam Hussein in Karbala and lost seven of his sons in the battle. After the battle, Hussein's successors showered Rahab Dutt and his community with sympathy, gratitude, and tenderness. They conferred the title of 'Husseini Brahmins' to the group, honouring its participation in Imam Hussein's cause of truth and justice. This community is a part of a larger sect of Brahmins known as Mohyals.

Advised by Hussein's children to return to India, Husseini Brahmins first came and settled around Lahore, now in Pakistan. After 1947, many of them moved to various states of India. Several members of this small group can be found in Maharashtra, Kashmir, Rajasthan, and Delhi. Among celebrities, actors Lara Dutta and Sanjay Dutt and journalist Barkha Dutt are lineages of this unique group of people.

Husseini Brahmins have created special rituals to proudly mark their Islamic heritage. 'We symbolize the centuries-old bond shared by Hindus and Muslims in this part of the world,' says Colonel Ramsarup Bakshi (retd), a member of this community.

Prologue

Prophet Muhammad was among his chief disciples, preaching, when Archangel Gabriel came down to him from heaven with a message from God. After communicating with the Prophet, the archangel vanished, filling the surroundings with a celestial fragrance.

The strange visit left Muhammad grave and downcast.

The disciples were worried. Ignorant though they were of the content of the archangel's despatch, they were sure that it was something grim. So, they, too had tears in their eyes.

Muhammad, on observing the sorrowful faces of his devotees, asked, 'What are you weeping for? What has pained you so much?'

Each of the devotees, joining his hands in supplication, replied, 'Master, when the full moon has hidden behind the clouds or has paled at the brightness of daylight, how can the stars remain shining? We are your ardent followers. We cannot bear to see a sad expression on your glorious countenance. As long as *you* are sad, we are bound to be so. We can guess that it is not a gentle puff of breeze but a strong blast of wind that has hit our magnificent mountain—

that it is a major storm that has caused the upheaval in our great ocean. Master, please oblige your humble disciples by revealing what has happened.'

Gently, the Prophet revealed, 'The child of one among you will become a staunch enemy of my beloved grandsons, Hassan and Hussein. He will kill Hassan by poisoning him and slay Hussein with weapons.'

Muhammad's followers were stunned! Rendered dry-mouthed, they could not utter a word for a while. Later, they said, 'Our master knows everything. Please tell us whose child is expected to commit that heinous crime. As soon as we come to know his name, we would take measures to prevent the tragedy. If you do not reveal the name of that future culprit's father, we will jointly kill ourselves by taking poison. Or, we will banish our wives, even if it is a sin to do so. We will stop looking at women's faces and never pronounce a feminine name.'

The Prophet said, 'Brothers! Nobody in the world can undo what God has willed. When He is writing a verdict, no mortal can stop His pen. What He orders cannot be reversed. Don't fret for what will happen in the future. And don't punish your wives for no fault of theirs. Our scriptures count that as a terrible sin.

'My announcing the name you fear is sure to hurt one amongst you. That is the reason why I wanted to keep it a secret. But since you insist on hearing it, listen. My esteemed Muawia will have a son who will be known to the world as Yazid. Yazid, growing up to become a grave enemy of Hassan and Hussein, will kill them.

'It is true that Muawia has not married yet. But that won't stop what God has proclaimed. God's might and skill defy definitions. And, He never fails.'

Muawia immediately promised in the name of his religion that not only would he remain single all his life, but he would also refrain from looking at a woman's face.

Prophet Muhammad said, 'Dear Muawia, this is God's will. And I know how much you trust Him. So, don't displease Him by vowing not to marry. That won't be right for a person like you. God is magnificently wise, infinitely glorious, and capable. Submit to His will.'

After such exchanges, the meeting was over. Taking their master's leave, the devotees went home.

A few days later, Muawia, after urinating, used a pebble to clean himself (as recommended by his religion where water is unavailable). The pebble, however, was composed of toxic particles, which severely infected his urinary tract. Muawia was in pain. In fact, his discomfort was so acute that it made him fall on the ground and writhe in agony.

Days passed by, but Muawia did not recover. On the contrary, his sepsis turned worse. The news of his misfortune spread among his friends. He was treated with all kinds of medicines, but, alas, in vain. People feared that Muawia would soon die.

When the news of Muawia's affliction reached Prophet Muhammad, he rushed to his devotee's side. Wanting to help him, the Prophet, taking the name of God, was about to blow over the affected part of Muawia's body. But before he could do so, Archangel Gabriel appeared again. 'O, Muhammad, beware, beware!' said the archangel. 'Don't try to abate that illness by taking God's name. Your efforts will be futile, as God has other designs regarding it. Muawia will recover only if he sleeps with a woman. Nothing else in this world can give him relief.' Delivering his message, the archangel vanished.

Prophet Muhammad called his followers, 'Brothers, there is no medicine for Muawia's illness. But he can still do something to cure himself. He can take a woman. If he agrees to have a woman with him, he will be saved.'

When the patient strongly objected to having a woman with him, the Prophet accused him of intentionally preparing to kill himself, ignoring the fact that suicide was a major sin.

In the end, it was decided that Muawia would lawfully marry an eighty-year-old lady and live together with her. After that marriage, Muawia recovered as Muhammad had predicted.

To understand the logic of the infinitely merciful Almighty's ways is beyond the power of mortals. Muawia's wife, however old, conceived and gave birth to a male child. Muawia had resolved to kill his own offspring if it was a boy, but as soon as he set eyes upon the newly born, his hatred melted and his heart filled with fatherly love. Muawia came to deem the child dearer than his own self. Instead of killing him, he was ready to sacrifice his own life for the child, if needed. And, as days passed, the father's love for his son grew in intensity. Only occasionally did he remember the terrible forecast about his son's future role in life and was genuinely saddened.

Sometime later, Muawia sought Prophet Muhammad and honourable Ali's permission to let him settle down with his family in the city of Damascus. 'I have not forgotten what has been predicted about my son, Yazid,' he said. 'My going away to Damascus with him will help him keep away from young Hassan and Hussein.'

It was Hazrat Ali who had fought and won the city of Damascus. But, large-hearted that he was, he had no hesitation in cheerfully giving it away to Muawia, a brother from his extended family. Prophet Muhammad said, 'Dear Muawia, let alone Damascus, even if you leave this world and go to another, what God has decreed will come about.' Those words shamed Muawia, but not enough to make him change his plans. In a few days, he left Medina and, with his family, moved to Damascus. There, enthroned as the ruler, he governed the domain well and spent long hours in prayers.

Prophet Muhammad left for his heavenly abode at seven in the morning on Monday, the twelfth of Rabi-ul-Awal (the third month of Hijri calendar) in the Hijri year eleven. Only six months later, in the same Hijri year, Bibi Fatima (the Prophet's daughter, Hassan and Hussein's mother and Hazrat Ali's wife) went to heaven, leaving behind her husband and sons. Hazrat Ali died in the Hijri year forty on Sunday, the fourth of Ramadan (the ninth month of Hijri calendar). On Hazrat Ali's passing away, the throne of Medina came to the great Imam Hassan, who ruled his kingdom with religious fervour and piety. In the meantime, Yazid had grown up in Damascus. What happened next follows hereafter.

(المخيم الحسيني)

Muharram Parva
The Story of Muharram

Chapter I

'Dear Son, my only child,' said Muawia to Yazid, 'I have come to you today, especially to say how much I love you and how keen I am to give you all that I possess. All my riches, my vast kingdom, and its large army are at your service. The crown of Damascus will soon be yours. You will rule over millions of people, protecting them and guiding them according to the beneficial principles of our national religion. Your subjects will adore you. Tell me, then, what is it that you still desire? What is it that still makes you unhappy? I don't know what troubles you. I watch you spending time aimlessly or going to evil places in a miserable mood, wasting your energy and ruining your health. Sometimes I feel that you have immersed yourself in an ocean of sorrow, determined to kill yourself with melancholy. What is the reason for all this? I am your father. Don't keep any secrets from me. Tell me everything. If it is money that you want, my entire treasury is open for you. Tell me, do you wish to have the throne immediately and be crowned the ruler of the people? If so, I can attire you in regal garments and perform your coronation. What greater joy can there be for me than to see you a king before I die! You are my jewel of a son, my tree of hope budding and flowering out of season.* Beloved, your downcast eyes upset me greatly. Please bare your heart to me. Holding your hands in fatherly affection, I entreat you to relate to me the reason of your grief.'

Yazid heaved a deep sigh. He wanted to say something, but his voice choked and his tongue felt heavy. The enchantment that had taken hold of him prevented him from confiding the truth to his father. He *did* utter 'zai', but so softly that his father could hardly hear it. It seemed that a part of that tiny sound was washed away by his tears, which soaked his cheeks and chest. Watching his son weep, thus, Muawia felt helpless.

The fire that burns outside a human body can be quenched with water, but the fire of amour, when burning within a person, has no water to quench it, even though it creates water in the form of tears. And, with no water to quench it, that fire of passionate love blazes with greater and still greater power. Yazid was not pining for a kingdom or an army. Nor was he desirous of a crown or a throne. His father had no idea, no inkling of the nature of his son's longing. Tears dimmed his vision as he urged again, 'Yazid, please tell me what is it that you want. I shall get it for you with money, power, skill, or cunning. You wander about the forest like a being possessed. I fear that you will be tempted to take your own life one day. Am I to remain alive to shroud and bury you, my own son?'

---

* According to legend, Muawia did not choose to marry any young girl but had wedded an eighty-year-old woman to avoid having a child. However, she had given birth to Yazid even at that age. Muawia, it is said, did not want a child of his own in order to keep the throne of Damascus free for Muhammad's grandson Hassan without any other claimant.

Hands joined in respectful address, Yazid answered, 'Dear Father, my sorrow is fathomless and there is no remedy for it. I am not an idiot. I know that money and power are not lacking in our lives. But I am so intensely struck by a tantalizing image of perfect beauty that there is nothing but agony for me. I would have told you what to do if there was a way of abating my torture. But, alas, my anguish cannot be calmed! Father, I cannot tell you more. I had kept all this to myself for a long time. Today, you commanded me to open my heart. I have dutifully revealed to you as much as is possible for me to do. I cannot speak any more. May be, someday soon, as you said, you will find me dead by taking some kind of poison. Only then, in the holy land of eternal bliss, shall I be at peace.'

While the conversation between the father and the son was drawing to a close, the elderly queen, supporting herself on a golden stick, entered the room and stood near them. Yazid rushed to welcome her and kissed her feet. He touched his father's feet too, and took his leave.

The ruler of Damascus, greeting his queen, assisted her to a seat. 'Attending to your advice,' he said, 'with the greatest of care and tenderness, I tried to make him open up to me, but failed. In the end, he began to weep and made me weep too. He is not pining for the kingdom or any otherworldly possession, and yet declares that his wish can never be fulfilled. Then, what he whispered softly filled me with shame! It seems that a seductress of extraordinary allure has put him under her spell.'

The ancient queen, lifting her head with an effort, spoke in a trembling voice, 'O, Great King! After making much enquiries, I have come to know, for sure, what ails Yazid. I can tell you what it was that Yazid had hinted at when he spoke to you. I guess you are acquainted with Abdul Zabbar?'

'That I am. I have indeed known him for many years.'

'Zainab is the name of Abdul Zabbar's wife.'*

'I·wonder now…yes, Yazid *did* pronounce the sound "zai". Unfortunately, he could not tell me more. So, my lady, what has Bibi Zainab done?'

'Nothing but that our Yazid is madly in love with her. He pines for her all the time. He tells me that he would die if he cannot get her. And what is the use of *my* being alive if my only child dies!'

With a slight roughness in his voice, Muawia said, 'Now, what do you want me to do about this wretched affair?'

'Not much except saving my only son's life. While you are there to attend to me, who am I to do anything on my own?'

Muawia was about to leave the room moodily without answering his wife when she took his hand into hers and pressed it gently. Calmed a little by that gesture, he took his seat again and said, 'Let the sinners and their supporters in hell assist in this business, not me! And I do not even want to hear anything more of this. Don't you remember the punishment fixed for a man who covets another's wife? Our holy books predict that such a man shall go to *jahannum*, the worst of hells. The worldly penalty for such a crime is no less

---

* Zainab is also the name of Hassan and Hussein's sister, Fatima and Ali's daughter. Yazid's love interest Zainab should not be confused with *that* Zainab. Another name for Zainab, whom Yazid loved, is Urainav.

torturous. The law directs such a culprit to be beaten to death with red-hot iron rods. Has Yazid forgotten such holy orders? I am the king. My duty is to protect each of my subject's life, possession, dignity, and clan identity. I am answerable to God for all this. If I fail in my duty, He will send me to hell to be burnt into ashes and recover to be burnt again. If Yazid wants to destroy himself, let him go ahead. I shall never join him in his sin. Why once? Let him be destroyed a thousand times. I shall not shed even one drop of tear. On the contrary, I shall thank God for removing a sinner from this earth. Hello, my queen, had you expected me to commit sins to protect my son? That will be impossible.'

The aged queen held her husband's hand tightly and said, 'Look, my gracious master, our Yazid has fallen into a dangerous trap. Such a trap is known to work its power upon many upright persons. Hundreds of religious scholars and devout saints have been snared by such a condition— the condition of falling in love like our Yazid has. And even our holy books speak of love and its glory. Love is a part of human nature. O, Badshah Namdar! There is nothing novel in what Yazid is going through. If you have patience enough, I can recount to you numerous stories of love—even great stories which shall be remembered for all ages—where love has conquered all obstacles. When in love, a lover often forgets everything except his object of love. He may forget his parents, his family, and his religion. I doubt whether he can even remember God. What control can Yazid have over such an overriding phenomenon? What can I or even you do to check it?'

Muawia, who had calmed down considerably by that time, replied, 'I have nothing against a human being's capacity to love. But don't you agree that the sentiment Yazid allows himself to feel is a wrong kind of love?'

'I don't, my lord,' persisted the queen, 'for I realize that such intense love has to be pure. Don't be unnecessarily harsh on Yazid, my king. Remember what he means to us. Remember what people do to get a son. They pray to God, they pray to holy men and saints. They give huge donations to the poor. Intending to have a worthy son, they exert themselves in all kinds of pious deeds. Yet, our son Yazid was born without asking. You did not want a son and I had not offered my blood to God desiring a son, thinking I was too old for that. And yet, the merciful Almighty has given us our Yazid—a miraculous gift! Think of all this before you despise him. I know how much you love him. I know you wish to have him near you all the time and you cannot be done with looking at his face. Once, years ago, you had intended to kill him, but failed. The sword had fallen from your hands and, instead of hurting your baby, you sat him on your lap and covered his cherubic face with hundreds of kisses.'

Softened, Muawia asked, 'Is there a way to help him out now?'

'Obviously, we have to do something to save Yazid's life without going against our religion or creating any social disgrace.'

'Sure. But I don't know how. In fact, if we can manage to abide by our religious laws and yet save our child, it will be enough for me. I don't care for social sanctions. In any case, people's preferences are fickle. Someone who blames you today can suddenly become your admirer tomorrow.'

The queen softly began, 'I have a plan. And I promise to execute it with the help and guidance of Marwan. You do not have to do anything except allowing us to carry on. We shall do nothing against our religion. In case you feel that we are doing so, or going against the rules laid by the leaders of our faith, tell us and we will stop immediately.'

The great king kissed his queen's hand and said with much satisfaction, 'I shall be really pleased if you can do as you say. God only knows how deeply saddened I am at Yazid's sufferings. If your strategy works, Yazid will live and I shall be left in peace to pray to my God.'

The queen nodded her head, indicating that everything would be done to the king's satisfaction. The particulars of the scheme, however, remained unsaid. And though she did not speak further, her gestures pointed out that the deal was settled.

Chapter II

By and by, the gist of the plan was laid before the king, and the two royal personages, the king and the queen, reflected on it. Yazid was then summoned to join in the discussions and he himself finalized the details of the plot. The venture was flagged off by sending a *kasad* to Abdul Zabbar.

A *kasad* is a cultured, dignified, gentle, and pleasant person. Renowned Muslim authors have portrayed the status of a *kasad* as distinguished in society. The profession of a *kasad* is not as humble as an ordinary messenger or courier of letters in today's Bengal. I make this point clear to convey to you that a very efficient and resourceful agent was sent to Abdul Zabbar from Yazid.

Abdul Zabbar was a well-to-do merchant, but yearned for more wealth. However, his wife Zainab was totally content with what her husband had. She was humble, meek, gentle, chaste, and pious and adored her husband, even though he was unattractive and ugly. She believed that serving her husband was her only means to reach heaven. She occupied herself with religious duties and often advised her husband to stop being greedy and jealous—for Abdul Zabbar was indeed jealous of Yazid's affluence. 'God has given each of His creatures exactly as much as it needs,' Zainab told her husband. 'Be satisfied with what you have. Look around you. You are better off than most of your neighbours. Be grateful to the Almighty who is omniscient and does what is the best for each one of us. Submit to His will and His justice.'

Abdul Zabbar did not like such speeches. According to him, happiness depended on money and he was always thinking of ways to augment his fortune. He came home only to eat. The rest of his waking hours were spent in the marketplace among other traders, looking for profitable business deals.

One afternoon, Zainab had prepared a delicious meal for her husband and laid it with gentle care before him when he came home. Sitting nearby, she fanned him quietly while he ate. The day was hot and she was moist with sweat, the clothes sticking to her body. Beads of perspiration glistened on her brow. Her face, hands, and garments were soiled with ash from the cooking fire. The natural heat of their scorching locality adding up to the heat of the stove had reddened her countenance.

Observing her for a while, Abdul Zabbar said, 'Dear Zainab, I think you are mistaken when you tell me to be content with what God has given me. I find that He has distributed His graces quite thoughtlessly. Otherwise, why would I lack the means for providing good servants for you? You are too delicate for this heat and for this never-ending housework.' Abdul Zabbar had a mirror with him, which he held up to his wife's face and added, 'See how you look right now.'

Zainab took the mirror from her husband's hand and, putting it aside, said, 'I love my work. What more can a woman like me need?'

'But if I were rich, I wouldn't have let you work. I wouldn't make you suffer like this.'

'Perhaps, you think that servants, jewels, and expensive clothes can make a woman happy. It is not so. Happiness is a spiritual experience.'

'I don't agree,' said Abdul. 'Money is the only source of happiness. If I were as wealthy as Yazid, I would have given you immense happiness. It is not my fault that God has not enough for me to spend on you.'

'It is good that you are not as rich or as powerful as Sheherzada Yazid. If you were so, you would not have loved a plain woman like me. With a higher position in society, you would have got attracted to prettier women. In fact, a change in social status can be an excellent test for detecting how steady a man is in his love. The husband who craves for money can even sacrifice his dearly loved wife for it.'

A little hurt by his wife's words, Abdul Zabbar said, 'It sounds like you are accusing *me* of being that kind of a person. However, all the wealth in the world cannot take away my love for you. Love is priceless and therefore cannot be bought at a cost.'

By then, Abdul had eaten his lunch. After washing, he collected his accounting ledgers and stationery. Wondering why his business assistant and kin Osman had not arrived yet, he was about to leave the house. At that very moment,

Osman rushed in. 'A *kasad* has come from Damascus!' he announced excitedly. 'He could get to this address only after a lot of enquiries and is quite tired. But he wants to see you immediately. I heard that he is carrying an ordinance for you from the king of Damascus!'

On hearing that, Abdul Zabbar made haste to meet the honourable gentleman waiting outside. In no time, they were facing each other. As was the norm of their society at that time, the eminent *kasad* praised the Lord of the Universe and the lord of Damascus before gently handing Abdul his letter from the High Command.

Abdul kissed the document again and again and raised it to his forehead before greeting its bearer with appropriate grace and gratitude.

Soon, Abdul entered his private quarters with the missive and began to read it. It said:

> Noble Abdul Zabbar,
> This is to let you know that our emperor, the ruler of
> Damascus, invites you to meet him. Come at once to
> his capital and accept his blessings.
>
> From
> Minister Marwan

Abdul was mesmerized by the sudden summon from his king and, considering himself extremely lucky, he said to Zainab who was close by, 'I wonder what good deed I have done to deserve a meeting with the Badshah. God knows what rewards are awaiting me!'

The neighbours were amazed at Abdul Zabbar's good fortune. They paid homage to their ruler, each touching the precious document to his forehead. Everyone spoke highly of Abdul. Congratulating him, his associates said, 'Dear Brother, don't forget to put in a good word for us when you are with the emperor.'

Abdul Zabbar collected his clothes—whichever were worthy enough to wear at the royal court—and engaged porters to carry them along. He arranged for his own transport too. He took leave of his neighbours and kinfolks, who were still singing his praises. He bade a gentle goodbye to Zainab, but was in a hurry to say anything more intimate to her. He was too excited with his sudden climb in status to remember her with any particular affection. But Zainab wept when her husband parted from her.

Chapter III

Every molecule in Yazid's body desired Zainab. She was in his thoughts during daytime and in his dreams at night. However, what mostly excited Yazid's intellect those days was not the emotion of love itself, but his plan of winning her as his own. He had a design for the purpose and was eager to use it. Could he really succeed in his endeavour? Was there a chance of failure? Such musings kept him nervous and made his countenance glow with fervour. That glow was mistakenly perceived as cheerfulness by the members of his household and his court. They were glad to think that Yazid had overcome his depression.

Marwan was not the chief minister of the kingdom, but he could usually do as he pleased because he was dear to Yazid. The actual chief minister Haman chose to leave Marwan alone due to his intimacy with the prince.

'O, Prince!' Marwan suggested to Yazid one day, 'you suffer so badly only because the king, your father, is alive!'

'True,' said Yazid, 'what freedom can a son have when his father is living? A son is supposed to always obey his father. That is the custom. I do not respect Hassan and Hussein. I do not bow my head when they are mentioned. My father gets irritated at that. It is awful! However, I am not yet ready to kill anyone to win my freedom. Besides making me unpopular in this life, the sin can hamper the quality of my life after death. Anyway, this time we are somewhat lucky as my father has given me a little allowance. He has promised not to intervene in the matter if our project falls within the religious boundaries. Hope this undertaking succeeds. If it does, we won't have to kill anybody and can avoid a major sin.'

Suddenly, merry tunes of music, the harbinger of good news, started playing. 'Cheering has commenced. Has Abdul Zabbar arrived already?' mused Yazid. He and Marwan hurried towards the royal court. They took a little time to reach there, but found to their relief that everything was in order. Every important officer had taken his respective position as per Yazid's directions. Soldiers stood in two neat rows, flanking the entrance to the court.

The well-mannered *kasad* who had returned from his mission abroad met Yazid and Marwan on their way to the court. Saluting them, he related, 'The emperor's order has been executed. Abdul Zabbar was given a ceremonious welcome and then ushered in to the head of state's private office.'

After a quick inspection of the public area of the court, the two friends entered Muawia's office to hear him converse with Abdul Zabbar.

Tense and alert, Abdul sat before the ruler of Damascus with joined hands, careful to maintain his good behaviour. Muawia spoke exactly as he was advised by his wife, who was in turn instructed by her son, Yazid. He said, 'Dear, Abdul Zabbar, I wish to have you close by me forever. Yet, I do not want to appoint you as an officer of the kingdom, for, if I do so, state politics with which you are unacquainted will become a burden on you. You may even make blunders out of your ignorance and become a laughing stock of the people here. I shall rather make you a part of my family so that you can enjoy your high status in peace and comfort.'

His hands still clasped together, Abdul said, 'My lord, I am only a humble servant of yours. I will do whatever you bid me to. The opportunity of sitting in front of you is in itself a great reward for me.'

Muawia continued, 'Abdul Zabbar, you will now hear from Marwan, the most important minister of my state, what I really wish you to do for me. I am late for my prayers. Let me take your leave now.'

After the sovereign had left, Marwan as his representative, addressing Abdul with great regard, said, 'Virtuous Abdul Zabbar, we humbly request you to become the husband of our beautiful and talented princess, Her Royal Highness Saleha, by formally marrying her according to holy laws. After your marriage, please become a permanent resident of Damascus. The emperor has already sanctioned large assets from his treasury for you to maintain a fitting social standing in this city.'

On hearing the extraordinary news, Abdul Zabbar was overwhelmed. What he had never dreamt of or imagined had happened! God can after all do anything! Tears of joy choked his voice, delaying his verbal acceptance of Marwan's offer.

Then, controlling himself, he said, 'O, Great Minister, I am very fortunate! I bow my head and submit to my lord's order.'

Marwan said, 'Your acceptance of our proposal gives us great pleasure. O, Abdul Zabbar, everything that will be required for an auspicious ceremony is ready. Let us then hold it in this assembly immediately. The time seems to be right.'

In a prearranged formation, clergy, royal staff, and family members of the king entered the premises at Marwan's signal. Festive melody began to play. The priest ordered Yazid to take on the duty of representing the bride. Marwan and Abdur Rahaman were formally sworn in as legal witnesses of Yazid's acceptance of that important duty.

At this point of my story, I would like to acquaint my non-Muslim readers to the salient features of a Muslim wedding so that they can grasp the significance of what is being recounted here.

In our community, no one from the groom's party is allowed to see the bride before a wedding. The groom, an adult male, has to recite a specific passage in Arabic, whatever his mother tongue be, addressing the guardians of the bride. A speaker from the bride's side has to respond to those Arabic words spoken by the groom. In essence, this constitutes the groom's proposal of marriage and the bride's acceptance of it. This contract, endorsed by two witnesses, is vital to a Muslim wedding. Reciting prayers or performing religious rituals are optional to this ceremony. A Muslim marriage can be contracted even without them.

I have said enough for my readers to understand the nuances of what my narrative will now gradually divulge.

However, let me take this opportunity to speak a little about the social ills of the Muslim dowry (*maharana*) system of our time.* Today, in India, lakhs and lakhs of rupees have to be given by the Muslim grooms to their brides.

Unfortunately, British law supports the arrangement. Consequently, the bride's side, falsely exaggerating the value of the assets promised by the husbands to their wives at the time of marriage, forces them to sell off whatever they have; sometimes, even their own ancestral property! We, the common Muslim men, are no less to blame. In our desire for securing the future of our daughters, we do not hesitate to demand excessive *maharana* from our sons-in-law-to-be. In contrast, the messenger of God, the glorious Muhammad and his family members, had charged practically nothing when giving away their daughters in marriage. My readers will be surprised to know that Hassan and Hussein's mother, honourable Bibi Fatima, received an amount of money at her wedding, which in today's rate of conversion would be four rupees and four annas!

Now to continue with my story:

The representative of the bride, along with the witnesses who vouched for his sincerity, left the court to go into the inner rooms of the palace to bring her genuine words of consent to marry Abdul Zabbar. Returning soon, they bowed before the assembly, as was the norm, before announcing their charge's message, 'Bibi Saleha is willing to accept this match, but on

---

* *Maharana* is opposite to what is usually understood by the word 'dowry'. According to this system, gifts are given by the groom to the bride at the time of their wedding.

a condition. She is aware that Abdul of Medina already has a wife named Zainab. The princess wants Abdul to lawfully divorce Zainab. If he does so, she would immediately accept him as her husband. She is also ready to donate a thousand gold coins to supplement the alimony that Abdul has to pay Zainab on divorcing her.'

On hearing such a preposterous demand, anybody would be distraught to think straight, at least for a while. But it seemed that Abdul remained thoroughly clear-headed even at that moment, for he made his decision instantly. 'I am ready to accept the condition. Why just in words of mouth? I can't wait to give my *talaknama* (declaration of divorce) in writing.'

Pen and paper were supplied to Abdul on the spot. In the names of Allah and his Prophet, Abdul Zabbar divorced his virtuous, devoted, and blameless wife. Many of the other gentlemen surrounding him rushed to sign their names below Abdul's signature as witnesses.

The document certifying the divorce was carried indoors to Saleha.

Ministers and their assistants waited patiently in the assembly for Saleha's reaction, while joyous music played on to entertain them.

What Zainab had feared when her husband had left her to meet the emperor had come true. Premonitions of an unknown danger strummed in her mind back in Medina, and her eyes were heavy with crying. Indeed, I have no words to describe the poignancy of her distress.

Saleha's representative returned from her quarters and, formally greeting the court, said, 'In this congregation, ministers, companions, and assistants of the monarch, as well as his relatives are present. In the name of God, let me reveal to them the exact words the princess has sent with us, "A person who is ready to abandon his innocent wife simply to rise in his own status or to satiate his hunger for more wealth does not deserve my hands. I am stunned at the treachery of a husband who cannot care for a beautiful relationship and is capable of forgetting his beloved wife so easily. I absolutely refuse to marry such a person and reject his proposal entirely.'"

Everybody in the milieu praised Saleha's wisdom and good sense. Abdul felt as if a thunderous sky had fallen on him. His plant of fantasy was struck by lightning, its flowers wilting in an instant. The princess's servants brought to Abdul the money promised by her as an additional alimony for his ex-wife. Abdul left it untouched. And, hiding himself in the crowd, he slipped out of the assembly and left the city. Discarding his fancy clothes for a beggar's raiment, he wandered in the woods without any intention of returning home.

Abdul's story spread far and wide. Even before his hired porters returned to his homeland, his neighbours had heard of it. In fact, the general public did not hesitate to exaggerate Abdul's unkindness when they spoke of it. Zainab heard one such version, but still hoped for it to be a rumour. But when the porters returned to confirm the tale, she was devastated. Concealing her distress deep inside her heart, she sent a message to her father to take her back in his household and soon started for her journey there.

Chapter IV

Amessenger was running swiftly through the desert. He had not stopped to rest for hours. Yazid, his master, had bid him to make his dispatch speedily. 'Tarry a little when you are too tired or thirsty or when you need to eat. But make up for the lost time as soon as you start to move again,' Yazid had ordered.

Moslem, for that was the name of the messenger, passed through the sandy terrain, panting through its heat. A person unaccustomed to such surroundings would be unable to traverse through it. Fortunately, Moslem belonged to that place. Being well informed, he was acquainted with its mountains and streams. He knew where to find clean water. Exhausted and dry-mouthed, he advanced towards a small hillock. Under the shade of the hillock was resting a tiny band of travellers who knew Moslem. Akkas, their leader, greeted him.

'O, Moslem! Where are you going, Brother?'

'Let me quench my thirst, O Akkas, before I answer you,' said Moslem.

'Water is close by. Look at those lush date palms. A clear stream of gently flowing, cool water is available there. Come, let us all go and sit there for a while.'

Reaching the palm grove, Akkas lifted a boulder to expose the stream of water he knew to bubble there. Filling his water bottle, he offered it to Moslem along with a fistful of dry fruit from his pocket. Moslem accepted them thankfully. Refreshed, he said, 'Brother Akkas, I am carrying Prince Yazid's marriage proposal to Lady Zainab.'

'What! Is Abdul Zabbar dead!' exclaimed Akkas, who was among the few people in the region who had not heard of Zainab's fate.

'No, but he has divorced his wife,' said Moslem.

Akkas was shocked. 'How could Abdul abandon such a beautiful and devoted wife?' he asked. 'There are few women in this region as gentle and chaste as Zainab. How cruel of Abdul to banish her! I did not expect this from him.'

'Brother Akkas, it is God's will,' reflected Moslem philosophically. 'The reasons behind why, when, and how something happens are beyond the capacity of our mental prowess. The Omniscient Mover of the Universe does what He thinks to be right.'

'For how long are they divorced?' enquired Akkas.

'Just a few days.'

'Which means that even the iddat* is not over?'

'It is so indeed, but that does not restrict another man from sending her a marriage proposal or her accepting it. The actual wedding can take place later.'

'Then, Brother Moslem, do me a favour. Do play the role of *my* messenger, too. First, put Yazid's proposal before Zainab and then mine. Even though there is scarcely a

---

* Days of mourning for a widowed or divorced woman.

chance of Zainab accepting me against Yazid, please don't forget to tell her that I, too, desire her as a wife. Yazid as a prince is more deserving, but I shall not extinguish my hope for her yet, for hope keeps a man going. And who knows? The Almighty might even influence her mind and make her want me. Anyway, please do not forget to present to her my sincere proposition. I beseech you in the name of the merciful God.'

Soon after the conversation, the two friends, taking each other's leave warmly, started on their separate courses. A little way onwards, Moslem met the honourable Imam Hassan with his hunting party, ready for an excursion.

Hassan had recently acquired the throne of Medina and was made the leader of his people. He waved to Moslem to come closer to him and was about to give him an affectionate hug when Moslem bowed low and kissed his feet. Then, joining his hands respectfully, he stood before the great man in silence. Sheherzada Hassan said, 'O Moslem, why be so formal and polite? Aren't you my childhood friend? Feel free to tell me whatever you want.'

Moslem said, 'You are the keeper of our faith now and represent the spiritual as well as the material world for us. Only at your feet can Muslims find their release from sin. Kissing them is one of our most sacred acts. Every Muslim now feels devoted to you and wishes to serve you. We are always eager to listen to your sermons. I am now just a lowly servant of yours and consider myself blessed if I can be of any use to you.'

'But I know that my meeting with you is a lucky omen,' said the Imam. 'This is a very good morning for me, as I have met my childhood friend after years. I am sure our hunting will be a success today. But Moslem, where are you going in such a hurry?'

'I am carrying Yazid's marriage proposal to Lady Zainab. Hazrat Muawia has ordered me to get her reply as swiftly as possible.'

'I have heard how Yazid tricked Abdul Zabbar into divorcing his wife. Perhaps, Hazrat Muawia was forced to take Yazid's side, or maybe he was kept in the dark about Yazid's real intentions. Yes, I have heard of the various opinions people have about the incident.'

'And now, Sir, even Akkas wishes to marry Bibi Zainab. He has urged me in the name of God to apply for him, after Yazid, as wanting to marry her. God knows whom she will choose between the two.'

Hassan smiled, 'If that is the case, can you carry my entreaty to her, too, O Moslem? I am a poor man, but please plead for her hand on my behalf. Let me be the last of the three of us proposing to her through you. Women generally love to have rich, good-looking husbands. I am neither handsome, nor wealthy. Yazid is both. Even Akkas is rich and charming. There is no denying that their claims on her are stronger than mine. Zainab is a jewel among women and she deserves the best. Yazid's or Akkas's household can give her all the respect and earthly comforts she deserves. I have only spiritual joy to offer her if she becomes mine.

'You know the condition of my life,' Hassan continued, 'Even though the throne of Medina belongs to me, I am practically a beggar. My family and I live a frugal life. The only wealth we have is devotion to God. Our only happiness is in serving Him. As such, I can hardly offer Zainab any worldly pleasures. Present my humble proposal, therefore, after the two more merited offers. And I shall eagerly wait for you to bring her reply. On your way back, please don't forget to tell me whom she chose.'

In a little while, the two old friends, bidding each other a gracious good day, took their separate ways.

As Moslem trudged on, he kept thinking of Zainab and the three men in love with her. He knew how passionately Yazid wanted her. The moment Yazid had looked at her face, which was as elegant as a gleaming moon, she became the centre of his world. He pronounced Zainab's name again and again all to himself, as if it were his string of prayer beads. Yazid was completely caught in the charm of her personality. Akkas was one of the richest men Moslem knew and was renowned for his good looks too. And even he wanted Zainab. The third person to want her was Imam Hassan himself! Imam Hassan, who could release all Muslims from sin, whose grandfather gave Muslims their immortal faith and revealed to them the true nature of God, requested Zainab's fair hand! How fortunate is demure Zainab! The messenger moved on and on, musing on such thoughts.

Chapter V

In a Muslim community, upon losing a husband, a woman's mourning lasts for four months and ten days. During that period, she is forbidden to wear fine clothes or apply cosmetics and perfumes on her body. She is also required to sleep on the floor without making a bed. Zainab was diligently observing all the ritualistic hardships to mourn her divorce. She spent most of her time in prayers, totally submitting her ego to the will of God.

Zainab was deep in prayers when Moslem reached her quarters, bearing messages for her.

A Muslim girl who was not a minor was free to accept or reject a proposal for her marriage. But custom required that she spoke of this matter—or any other matter—with a male outsider only in the presence of a family member. So, her father stood nearby as Moslem addressed Zainab and said, 'O, Pious Lady, I have come to you as soon as I could make myself presentable after my long journey. Let me, then, at once impart the messages I was delegated to bring. We know that your period of mourning is not over. But that does not hinder another man from proposing to you. I have come from Damascus where Emperor Muawia rules in all his splendour. Lord Muawia's only son Yazid requests your hand in marriage. There is no doubt that Yazid will soon become the owner of a vast estate. And, as Yazid's wife, you are sure to become the chief queen of his kingdom—lavished with finery and delectable food.

'However, besides Yazid's marriage proposal, I also carry other messages for you. On my way from Damascus, I met Akkas, one of the favourite associates of gracious Muhammad. He, too, begs you to be his wife. God has given him the finest of physiques that men can boast of, and he is exceedingly wealthy.

'Lastly, the glorious Muhammad's daughter Bibi Fatima and Hazrat Ali's elder son Hazrat Hassan is also keen to be your husband. But compared to Yazid, he is a poor man. Neither does he have a dazzling palace, nor a powerful army. Being his wife can never give you any material comfort.

'Gentle lady, these are the three marriage proposals I bring for you and have presented them to you in the most unbiased manner. With your own free discretion, please choose one of them.'

On patiently hearing Moslem's address, Zainab spoke in a soft and gentle voice, 'Yes, I shall be taking a new husband when my period of mourning is over. But, at the moment, it gives me pain to even think of a married life. Yet, since my father bids me to speak about the proposals you have brought for me and because you expect a ready answer from me, I shall bare my heart. I have no idea why God has created me, but He must have some purpose or use for it. Let Him fulfil that purpose through me by making me endure whatever He plans for me. I humbly submit to His will with all my heart's gratitude. How short is our life! It is over as soon as we close our eyes in death. Why should we fill the short span of time that life is with crooked ambitions? Wealth, power, or charming looks cannot satisfy me, for people with such assets are like empty shells, lacking in their hearts the true love for God. I was never greedy for money and positions and never will be. This is the message from the depth of my heart.'

Moslem said, 'But you have still not told me whom you finally accept.'

'My intention cannot be clearer,' replied Zainab sweetly. 'When the master of our spiritual and material world wishes my services, who else can be a happier woman than I? And it is well known that the world was created on account of that holy man's maternal grandfather. Hazrat Adam, our very first ancestor, at his first conscious moment, had witnessed the name of Hazrat Muhammad heading a list of great names written below God's supreme seat. How can I refuse the call of that magnificent Muhammad's grandson? His company will be like heaven for me! There are many ways to atone for one's sins, but the best way is by being blessed by a holy man. The fire of hell ceases to burn for such a blessed person, and heaven's gate opens wide for him or her.

'I have nothing more to tell you but that, as soon as my mourning period is over, I shall be ready to serve Hazrat Hassan as his wife. There is no place for any other man in my heart.'

Moslem said, 'I salute you, Lady Zainab! Your greatness will be remembered for generations to come. How easily you have banished the temptations of wealth, comfort, power, and good looks! You truly value the untarnished joy of eternal heaven and can give up everything for that. Now, please bid me adieu and allow me to return to Damascus.'

On his way back home, Moslem met Hassan and then Akkas and imparted Zainab's avowal. Then, musing on various matters, he hurried towards his abode.

Chapter VI

Yazid was counting the days for Moslem's return. When the expected day dawned, according to his calculations, he anxiously waited for the sun to set, thinking that Moslem would arrive in the evening. However, seven more evenings passed after that without any sign of Moslem.

The fact was that Yazid's calculations were wrong. He had imagined Moslem to take only half the time he would actually need on his journey. The delusion was typically the symptom of a lover's angst and should not be criticized too harshly. Even though time is priceless, a passionate lover wishes it to fly twice or thrice as fast when he awaits his beloved's news to be brought to him. Conversely, when the lover and his beloved are together in happiness, the lover wishes the day to prolong like a seemingly unending day in Lapland. Alas! Time moves on steadily at its own pace, ignoring individual preferences.

The separation from Zainab was a torture for Yazid. His mind was overcrowded with a variety of sensations, which he could share only with his best friend Marwan. And yet, even Marwan was away at that time. Longing for Zainab had almost paralyzed Yazid. Even though Muawia, his father, was

critically ill with little hope of recovery, Yazid rarely went to
his bedside.

Yazid had seen Zainab once without her knowledge. She
was smiling then, her rosy lips slightly parted. Two simple
jewels hung from her ears. A piece of pearl filigree lacing
her hair and gently touching her forehead had enhanced
the innocence of her faultless profile. Its soft lines seemed
ethereal. Yet, the tips of her eyebrows were sharp and had
struck Yazid's heart like two arrows. Yazid was smitten badly.
The glow of Zainab's vision did not fade in his memory, even
after the dimming effect of many successive nights of sleep.

Yazid would hear of Zainab as soon as Moslem came
back. How enchanting those first few moments of her news
would be! He would make Moslem repeat over and over again
her joyful words consenting to his proposal. He would urge
Moslem to relate every minute detail of their happy exchange
of words. And, later, how would he spend the first conjugal
night with her? What name would he call her? Would Zainab
be amused to hear how he had invented Saleha, a non-
existent sister, only out of his desperation to be with her? Or
should he hide from her that bit of treachery? Such thoughts
of a seemingly useless nature kept Yazid agitated. A day
came when he even forgot to take his supper. His servants,
waiting for him to finish his meal, sat at a distance, cursing
him in irritation.

Marwan, who often visited Yazid at odd hours, came to
soothe his friend. 'Why are you so worried, Prince?' he asked.
'There is not a shadow of doubt now that Zainab will be
yours. Women, I know, are crazy for wealth. When offered,

which woman can resist the temptation of becoming your chief queen? Be sure that Zainab will accept you.'

'I know that,' said Yazid. 'Only the long wait for her feels unbearable. She has yet to go through her share of mourning.'

'Be patient, Prince!' urged Moslem. 'The harsh hours of separation will soon pass. Her period of mourning will, no doubt, come to an end by and by.'

At that moment, the queen's personal maid hurried into the room and said, 'O Prince, the emperor, your father, wants to see you immediately!' Asking Marwan to stay back, Yazid followed her to his father's bedchamber.

Muawia lay in his sickbed with his wife sitting next to him, worry and concern writ large on her face. Yazid touched her feet and took a seat very close to his father, who softly uttered, 'Moslem has come back (Yazid looked all around, but could not see Moslem in the room) and has made me proud of young Zainab. Her calm and consistent faith in God, her patience and devotion to truth, and her superiority of mind at such a tender age have surprised me. Anybody would be impressed with her qualities. God is sure to punish Abdul Zabbar for hurting this innocent child.'

Yazid could not fathom why his father was praising Zainab in that manner. 'Perhaps,' he ventured to think, 'my father is instructing me to take good care of her when she becomes my wife.' Yazid was eager to hear more about his future spouse. However, he could not understand his mother when she pronounced in a tone of displeasure, 'Many girls are as good-looking and as devoted to God as her.' Yazid was a little hurt. Was his mother already jealous of Zainab?

'There might be other beautiful and religious women in the world, but none can be as wonderful as Zainab,' Muawia replied to his wife. 'The proof is right here,' he went on. 'Look, how easily she has rejected the temptations of wealth, beauty, and royal grandeur. How readily she has accepted the proposal of only *that* suitor who can give her freedom and peace in life hereafter.'

Yazid was quick to ask, 'Of whom are you talking about, Father?'

Muawia replied, 'Why? He is the great Muhammad's grandson, respected Ali's son, Hassan. The person whom you hate so much that even hearing his name makes you sick. But Zainab, with her exquisite feminine sensitivity, with great pleasure, has consented to be Hassan's wife. Dear Yazid, abandon your anger and hatred for Hassan and Hussein. Give up those cheap sentiments and seek the true path of heaven in the glorious light of your ancestral faith. Mind your worldly duty, too, by serving this small kingdom as a just ruler. My days are over. Be my deserving heir. Be more submissive and cooperating to Ali's sons than even I have been. Always remember that they are our superiors.'

Muawia paused. But words came rushing to Yazid's lips— angry words rudely objecting to his father's comments. 'I am the Prince of Damascus,' he began, 'my treasury overflows with wealth. I command a strong army. I live in the grandest palace of this region. I have everything that a man of my age may want. And yet, I was ready to give up all that— give up even my life for the sake of being with Zainab. How can Hassan marry her? How can I allow them to be happy?

Hassan is worthless and poor. Even his ancestors were such. They cannot even afford the fuel to light a single lamp in the evening or eat a decent supper. Do you expect me to respect Hassan, the head of such a filthy family? On the contrary, I am determined to take my revenge, for he has dared to steal away Zainab from me. Be assured that I am going to punish him and his family severely. Hassan has dared to hurt my feelings. My revenge will hurt his and his people's feelings a hundred times more. Sooner or later, if I am alive, I resolve to strike him hard.'*

Muawia, lifting himself up with an effort, cried in anger, 'O, Wicked Sinner! How dare you utter such words! Alas, what the great Muhammad had predicted has come true at last!**

'O, Fallen One, don't imagine yourself to be so grand! You are now fit to be the inmate of the lowest of hells, where you are dragging me with you! Alas that I had not killed you as soon as you were born! O, Sinner, you know that this prosperous kingdom is not ours. Ali had given it to me out of his kindness as a master humouring one of his obedient servants. How could you use such harsh words for that respected Ali's descendant? You wicked one, please leave me alone! I do not want to look at you.'

---

*   The battle of Karbala, on which *Bishad Sindhu* is based, was fought as a political power struggle. It came about when Yazid, the ruler of Damascus, wanted to crush a group of people who refused to acknowledge his authority. In his novel, however, Mir creatively explores a legend that hints at Yazid's love for a married woman and makes it the main cause of trouble.

**   Hazrat Muhammad, according to legend, had predicted that Muawia's son will kill Hassan and Hussein.

Yazid departed from the room grimly. His mother tried to console Muawia, 'Be patient, my lord!' she said, 'Don't be agitated. That will only slow down your recovery.'

'I don't care to live one moment after what I heard from Yazid. O, Merciful Almighty, please release me from this sinful house as quickly as you can!' Weeping and praying thus, Muawia fell back on his bed.

Chapter VII

Time never stops. By and by, Zainab's days of mourning were over. Hassan himself came over to where Zainab was staying and married her. Then he brought her home and introduced her to his family.

Hassan already had two wives and a son with his first wife, Hasnebanu. Abdul Kasem, Hassan and Hasnebanu's son, was by then a talented young man well-trained in weaponry. He assisted his father in all his activities. Some of his unique feats would be described later in my narrative. Kasem was also devoutly religious, as were most of the citizens of the holy city of Medina.

Zaida, Hassan's second wife, was still childless.

Anything with two or more focal points has to be complicated. A man with more than one wife has to bear up with an intricate married life. Hassan's first wife Hasnebanu was respected by all, even by Zaida, although she was not really happy to be a second wife. When Zainab came as Hassan's third wife, it was too much for her. She considered Zainab as her bitter enemy and was extremely irritated with Hassan for marrying a third time. Until then, Zaida dared to believe that

Hassan was deeply in love with her, but now she felt deceived. Though Hassan behaved with her just as he did before, Zaida imagined that the true fondness for her was now missing from his heart. She blamed Zainab's exceptional beauty for that and hated her. Her hatred for Zainab intensified as months passed. Hasnebanu, guessing the situation, took pity on Zainab and was always kind to her.

It must be difficult for a man to love two wives equally well. When there are three, having equal fondness for each, to my mind, would be almost impossible. I cannot explain, therefore, to my readers, why Hazrat Hassan took up such a challenge. However, my readers and I are ordinary mortals. With our limited mental and spiritual abilities, we should not even begin to judge the ways of great men. Hassan, moreover, could not be accused of breaking any religious laws, as our religion allows a man to keep up to four wives. And, out of his large-hearted gentleness, Hassan was always able to treat his wives with impartiality.

Apparently, therefore, there was no reason for Zaida to be so distressed, and yet her inflated ego could not reconcile with the situation. Could a woman have three husbands? No, because the husbands would not be comfortable sharing one wife. Why should a woman, then, be expected to be friendly with her sister wives? She brooded.

There are three types of enemies: the enemy proper, a friend's enemy, and an enemy's friend. By the same token, Hassan, once an object of Zaida's love, was gradually transformed by her warped sensibilities into a bitter enemy, as he was now the admirer of her enemy, Zainab.

News travelled from Damascus to Medina. Hassan heard how bitterly Yazid had reacted to his marrying Zainab and how Muawia rebuked his son for that. People feared, he heard, that Muawia would soon die, leaving Yazid in power.

Yazid had hated Hassan and Hussein since the time of their boyhood rivalries. Now that Yazid's idol was Hassan's wife, how furious he must be—wondered the Imam. He even spoke to Zainab about the matter. And yet, he was not prudent enough to foresee any harmful consequences of Yazid's jealousy reaching Medina. One reason for his casual attitude, of course, was that he thought that much of what he heard about Yazid loathing him was exaggerated.

Hassan's opinion of life was sublime. His happiness lay in worshipping the merciful Almighty. He had dedicated his being to religion. The pettiness of the mundane world did not interest him. He had no desire for wealth. It did not bother him that Medina, the province he ruled, was poor and weak. Fortunately, he had loyal subjects and that was his real strength. Medina's citizens would even give up their lives to advance the cause of Hassan and Hussein.

It was evening. Hassan, after performing his prayers, was taking a quiet stroll in front of the main mosque of the city, softly reciting the name of Allah again and again. Suddenly, his eyes fell on a fakir who came close by and saluted him. The fakir's tattered clothes, which also covered his head, were held in place with many knots. A string of stone prayer beads gleamed around his neck, as he stood holding his wooden walking stick.

'Master!' said the elderly fakir, 'I have something important to tell you. It is about a *kasad* whom I saw passing by while I was sitting on a hillock. I suddenly found him tumble down with the name of God on his lips. Worried, I came down from my perch quickly to attend to him and noticed that a steel arrow had struck him. In fact, it had penetrated his chest and was stuck on the rock behind him. Though bleeding profusely, the *kasad* was still alive and was trying to tell me something. What I understood from his disconnected words was that he was carrying a message from Emperor Muawia for you. The emperor, he said, was critically ill. Sir, probably in his message, he had invited you to meet him before he died.

'When I was, thus, bent over the wounded *kasad*, I heard the sound of a horse's hooves and, looking up, found Prince Yazid on horseback approaching towards us. Before the rider could discover me, I slipped behind a rock and, hiding there, watched his activities. Dismounting his steed, Yazid approached the victim and removed a piece of paper from a pouch in his belt. Mounting his horse again, he rode off speedily. I have nothing more to tell you, Sir!' concluded the fakir and moved away in a hurry.

Hassan reflected upon his strange visitor and his message. Who was he? Why was he so keen to describe to him his experience? And why did his appearance and style of speaking seem so familiar? It did not take long for Hassan to arrive at an answer. The odd-looking fakir was none other than Abdul Zabbar! How cruelly fate can change a man's condition!

Hassan was concerned about Muawia's indisposition. Should he go and visit him? He hurried homewards to discuss the matter with his younger brother, Hussein.

Chapter VIII

M uawia's illness had worsened. He was totally confined to bed. Since the unfortunate confrontation with his son, he had not set his eyes upon him. And his resolve of not seeing him was still as strong as ever. He was determined to hand over his kingdom and all its assets to Hassan and Hussein, who, as Ali's sons, were believed to be the rightful owners by many in the community. He had sent a *kasad* to bring them over to Damascus, wishing to meet them before he died. As the estimated time for their arrival had passed, Muawia was worried and restless.

No one in Damascus except Yazid knew that an accident had befallen that messenger.

Muawia shared his anxieties with his trusted chief minister, Haman. 'Dear Haman, what do you think has happened to our *kasad*? Why hasn't he brought Hassan and Hussein to me yet?'

Haman replied, 'Master, I am certain that on hearing about your illness, the two brothers would have rushed to your bedside. It seems that they have not received your message— that our *kasad* was somehow unable to reach them.'

Though Yazid had not visited his father since their row, he had pierced a secret opening into the sickroom. Through it, he had continually spied on his father to know in advance of whatever he was planning for the future. So, one day, Yazid was listening when Muawia said, 'O Haman, what curse has come upon my beloved land! I fear that our *kasad* has met with some accident. Let us send another messenger to Medina, and this time we must send Moslem again. He is my most trusted and efficient *kasad*. O Haman, let Moslem carry a letter from me to Hassan and Hussein. Write to them on my behalf that I am about to die and that I am restless to see them for the last time. Also, request them to take possession of Damascus, their ancestral kingdom. I am tired of looking after it. (At that point of Muawia's delivery, Yazid slipped away soundlessly from his hidden place.) I suspect that wicked tricks are being played around us. Send Moslem to Medina under total secrecy. Let no one know about his whereabouts.'

Haman took his leave and, in a short time, as per the king's orders, sent Moslem to Medina.

Moslem, a devoted servant of Muawia, was also a disciple of Hassan. Panting, he ran and ran therefore with Muawia's message to Medina, as if his was a sacred mission. Crossing the city boundary, he entered a vast desert. The hot sand scalded his feet, but he did not care. His only aim was to reach Medina at the earliest. At places, mounds of sand stood high. Some of the mounds had solidified into rocks after remaining fixed in one place for months. Moslem was passing such a sand dune on his right when four masked men with arms emerged from behind it and surrounded him.

'Who are you?' Moslem asked. 'Why are you stopping me?'

One of his captors replied in a deep voice, 'Consider yourself lucky, man, that you are designated as a *kasad* today. Otherwise, we would have chopped off your head by now.'

'Leave me alone!' shouted Moslem. 'I am carrying a royal message for respected Hassan and Hussein. How dare you intercept me in my imperial duty?'

As he spoke, Moslem took out his sword from its sheathe and swung it fiercely about. The villains stopped closing in on him, but one of them unmasked himself and said, 'Moslem, look who I am.'

Moslem glanced at him and instantly changed his posture. He threw his weapon on the ground and stood at attention, joining his hands in tribute to the speaker, for he was none other than the prince of Damascus, Yazid. As a loyal subject of the state, Moslem was bound to obey him.

At Yazid's orders, his companions searched their captive and stripped him of all his arms. Muawia's letter to Hassan and Hussein was torn to pieces by Yazid before he declared, 'While my father is living, you are to bid your time in isolation in a prison. I hear that you are a religious man. From now on, let your pious prayers be for Muawia's early death.'

Moslem was silent. He stood there like a statue while Yazid's men chained his hands and feet and put an iron ring around his neck. He walked slowly to where they were leading him. O, the doings of a selfish man!

Yazid blew his whistle to call another of his assistants, who was waiting with a horse for him behind another hillock. Mounting the horse, he rode back to town.

Chapter IX

The palace of Damascus was under a pall of gloom. Muawia's condition had turned critical. He had stopped speaking, and the pupils of his eyes had turned upwards. His wife, the queen, was feeding him spoonfuls of sweetened water. Muawia's attendants were in tears. Kinfolks, surrounding the sickbed, chanted the holy name of God.

Suddenly, heaving a deep sigh, Muawia uttered the sacred words, '*Lahellaha Ellalaha Muhammadar Rusullalaha*' (There is no God but Allah, and Muhammad is His messenger). At that, the sound of the collective prayer in the room heightened. People took hope. Perhaps, a miracle was happening. Perhaps, the emperor would be spared on that occasion.

But, alas, after calling the merciful Almighty's name once more, Muawia's lips stiffened. The lids of his eyes fluttered for a moment and shut forever.

The queen, placing her hand on the chest of her husband's body and finding no movement there, wept bitterly. The others in the room also began to wail loudly.

Exactly at that moment, riding on a horse, Yazid appeared at the yard outside. Dismounting quickly, he entered his father's room. Touching the dead body here and there to make sure that it was really devoid of life, he left as hurriedly as he had come—his eyes without a hint of tears.

Yazid returned to the scene of death shortly afterwards though, and took full charge of the funeral rites. The body was washed and wrapped in a clean piece of cloth and laid with great honour in the assembly for the public to pay their homage. Appropriate hymns from religious books were recited for the peace of the departed soul. Hundreds of faithful men gathered, even without invitation, around the covered body to raise their hands in prayers, pleading with the merciful God to bestow heavenly peace to the departed.

Thus, Muawia's role on the earthly stage came to a close. His persona was only a memory to his associates thenceforth.

Concerned about Muawia's illness, Imam Hassan and his brother Hussein were on their way to be at his bedside. They were about to reach Damascus when the news of his demise reached them. So, instead of proceeding further, they turned back for Medina, greatly saddened.

Muawia would never come back to Damascus. He would never set his eyes on his son. He would never rebuke him for any cruelty he might inflict on Hassan and Hussein. It was a great relief for Yazid as he succeeded to his father's throne and wore his crown. On the other hand, people loyal to Muawia—honest, just, and righteous people—were filled with apprehension. To what extent would Yazid's misconduct go without any check? They wondered.

Dear readers, at this point of my story, I feel that I have brought you at the very verge of *Bishad Sindhu*—a vast sea of melancholy.

Yazid became thus the totalitarian head of a sovereign state. Everybody was terrified of him.

The first job the new monarch set for himself was to call an assembly of all the aristocrats of his kingdom the very next day. As the day dawned, hundreds of gentlemen travelled to the palace to be on time for the meeting. Soon, there was a huge crowd at the court. At the stipulated moment, Yazid appeared dressed in finery and took his seat on the throne. Marwan, who was the de facto as well as the joint de jure prime minister of the domain, addressed the gathering thus, 'This day is a blessed one for us! A new ruler has ascended the throne of Damascus. As he is the most deserving successor to this throne and a capable administrator, let us all rejoice for a bright and fulfilling future for our country. The new king has brought a new, happy sunrise with him, and he would never let it set. Let us then welcome this novel era and salute its magnificent master.'

Everyone in the assembly bowed their heads in homage to Yazid. Marwan went on, 'Gentlemen, please allow me to announce something further. His Highness, the king, has taken the baton of law and justice in his own hands from today. He has chosen to put to trial today the very first accused of his reign—a dangerous traitor of our monarchy. In fact, all of you, Sirs, have been invited here to witness that dangerous enemy of our state being tried.'

At Marwan's signal, the security personnel brought the accused in front of the assembly. The noblemen were amazed to find that the chained prisoner was none other than Moslem. There was pin-drop silence in the hall as the spectators sighed in anguish. They could hardly believe their eyes! As one of the most favourite and trusted assistants of late Muawia, Moslem was a highly respected member of his community. It was surprising to see him come to such a pass so soon after his master's death. Muawia's body was still intact in his grave. Many of his friends were still formally mourning for him by wearing the simplest of clothes. Muawia's name was still at the tip of people's tongues. And yet, one of Muawia's beloved associates was being punished so brashly. How ruthless could Yazid be!

The crowd was silently praying for Moslem, though nobody dared to express aloud their sympathy. Moslem looked like a phantom. The stress of solitary confinement had taken its toll on him. He wondered at the presence of so many important people. Were they all gathered simply to watch his miserable state? He was in total control of himself though, ready to accept whatever was in store for him, for his conscience was clear. It was not a sin for a *kasad* to be loyal to his employer—and he had been only that—an obedient messenger of Lord Muawia, carrying his master's missive to Ali's sons. If Yazid chose to punish him for that, let him. He would never bow to that upstart young man and ask for his mercy. The noble *kasad* stood still, calmly submitting himself to the will of God.

Addressing the tense audience pitifully looking at Moslem, Marwan informed, 'The person standing yonder is a traitor, an enemy of our state. The hour of his trial has come. Kindly pay attention to the legal proceedings.'

It was then Yazid's turn to speak. He said, 'The accused you see there is a dangerous criminal. Anybody who thinks otherwise is also a criminal like him and a threat to our nation.'

The assembly remained anxious and sombre. Some of the gentlemen trembled in fear. People who had wished to speak up for Moslem gave up the idea.

Yazid continued, 'This schemer does not hesitate to tell a lie. Once, he was entrusted to carry my marriage proposal to Bibi Zainab. Instead of doing as he was bid to, he asked the lady to marry my bitter enemy, Hassan. This wicked creature is entirely responsible for getting Hassan and Zainab married. I am absolutely certain that Zainab was deliberately kept ignorant of *my* proposal to her. If she had known that I desired her, she would have instantly accepted me. Zainab is aware of Hassan's wretched living conditions. Yet, that scoundrel Moslem, giving her false impressions of Hassan's whereabouts, made him appear attractive to her. Listen, gentlemen, did I appoint Moslem to carry Hassan's message to that gentle lady? No, I didn't. Then why did he carry his message? Of course, because he wanted to work against me. Of course, he wanted to ruin me. And it is not that Moslem was unaware of my fondness for Zainab. Like everybody else in Damascus, he had watched me go mad to have her and desiring to die for her. How could he be so callous with my proposal to her then? How could he make her marry another man? What treachery can be worse than this? And there is more. His villainy against me continued. To dethrone me from my rightful position as the head of state, to devastate my life, to make me a beggar, he promptly agreed to carry Muawia's letter to Hassan in Medina, inviting him and Hussein to take control of our country. I order, therefore, that Moslem be slain. Let his head be cut off in front of me.'

Shaking with anger, Yazid proceeded to complete his sentencing, 'And I want my order to be carried out here and now, in this court!'

Joint chief minister Marwan had to intervene at that point. He said, 'Your Highness, your wish will surely be respected. But punishing a criminal in a public place is against the code of state administration....'

'Damn your state administration!' shouted Yazid. 'My orders are above all codes. Whoever opposes me will be punished with death—even you Marwan, if it comes to that, so beware!'

Hardly was the last sentence out of Yazid's lips when Moslem's bleeding head rolled off on the ground. The noblemen, witnessing the gory scene, stood stunned. Many felt giddy and blinded. The *kasad*'s bloody, headless body, entangled in prisoner's chains, lay at their feet. The blood it oozed—the honest blood of a trusted messenger of the late ruler—spoilt the sanctity of Damascus. The majestic dignity of the state built bit by bit by Muawia was stained. On the floor, streaks of blood wrote the message 'Yazid, this is not the end' in Arabic.

Yazid rose proudly from his seat and addressed the gathering again, 'Honourable ministers, officers of my army, and guests from other courtiers, Moslem's execution was an example for your advantage. Anyone in my kingdom who acts against my will shall be similarly punished.' Pausing for a minute, he continued, 'I am the head of a prosperous state.

I command a strong army. Hassan is nothing compared to me. And yet, he dares to marry a woman fit to be a queen—a woman who could have been happy only with me. I will show Hassan the consequences of such an idiotic behaviour. Not only will I spoil his marriage, but I will also destroy his life in every way. I will not rest before killing him and every member of his and Muhammad's family. Till the end of this world, let the devotees of Hassan and Hussein beat their chests for the deaths of those two brothers.'

Turning towards Marwan, Yazid ordered, 'Bring the letter that I had asked you to draft for Ali's sons. Read it out to this assembly. Let people who are fond of Muhammad's family know what is coming upon them.'

Marwan promptly took out the document from his folder and began to read it:

To Hassan and Hussein,

Are you not aware that Emperor Yazid, like the powerful sun of noon, is dominating our region? All the lesser kings with their states around Damascus have accepted him as their overlord. They have sent gifts to him or have met him in person to pay their respects. Each of them has also paid their individual taxes to Yazid. Mention your reason for not sending any contribution yet to the emperor's treasury from Mecca and Medina. I command you to come to Damascus immediately to kiss the throne of our empire and accept Yazid as your superior. Also, after reading this letter, remember to mention the new emperor's name in your Friday prayers.

Your failure to follow the above instructions will brand you as traitors of our empire.

From
Chief Minister Marwan

As soon as the letter was read out, it was dispatched to Medina through one of Yazid's trusted *kasad*s.

Yazid then declared the end of the conference. A large number of noblemen turned homewards with tears in their eyes.

Chapter X

Hassan, Hussein, and their friends Abdullah Omar and Abdur Rahman were sitting near the holy shrine of Muhammad, discussing a serious matter. They always went to that sacred place whenever they needed to meditate or reflect, or discuss or decide on important strategies. They also visited there to share their pious thoughts with other citizens of Medina. But what were they discussing that day? They looked worried. What possible danger were they afraid of? Dear readers, standing beside the fence of the shrine was the *kasad* from Damascus assigned to bring Yazid's message to Ali's sons. The sanctum sanctorum of the shrine was reserved only for people intimately known to Muhammad and their families. So, after delivering his letter at the gate, the messenger from Damascus was waiting outside. Next to Muhammad's tomb, the four friends were discussing the message they had just received. Omar exclaimed, 'How fast have things changed! Muawia was among the most sincere disciples of Hazrat Muhammad. He had submitted both his body and his soul to the guidance of the Prophet. It is hard to believe that Yazid, his son, has the temerity to demand taxes from you, the pious grandsons of Muhammad! Yazid has the insolence even of wanting his name to be recited in the Friday prayers! This is intolerable!'

Abdur Rahman added, 'Yazid has lost his mind! How else can he expect to collect taxes from Mecca and Medina, while you, I, and the other loyal citizens of the twin cities are alive? My advice to you, Sirs, is that Yazid must be severely punished for his meanness. To start with, this *kasad* must be rebuked and sent back with the letter he has brought. The sacrilegious words it carries have no place in holy Medina.'

Omar responded, 'You are right, Brother. What courage the rascal has! How dare Yazid communicate those words! How dare he gets them written on paper and sends them to us by a mere messenger! Didn't he have a higher-ranking official in his court? Have all people of consequence vanished from Damascus after Muawia's death?'

'Yazid is a beast,' said Abdur Rahman, 'who cannot value the company of good men. Haman, the good soul, has lost all his power. Yazid's favourite minister Marwan is the most important courtier in Damascus these days. Yazid depends on him for all his advice and guidance.'

Imam Hassan, who was listening patiently to his friends' exchanges, then spoke, 'No wonder it has come to this. I suspected, as soon as I read that letter, that it was not Yazid but someone else who was behind the mischief. Anyway, I suggest that we just return it to Damascus.'

Imam Hassan's younger brother Hussein, who had deeply felt the slight contained in the letter, said, 'Simply sending the thing back won't satisfy me. I want to really punish the crooks. Damascus belongs to us, as our respected father had conquered it. And now, those who were temporarily delegated the reign of the domain are claiming to be our superiors! This is preposterous! How can we accept this?'

The Imam urged, 'Be patient, Brother. We cannot afford to be rash. We have to think about all the possible consequences. To my mind, let us just return the letter this time and watch how Yazid reacts.'

'As always, I shall obey you, my elder brother. But I won't feel easy without, at least, giving a piece of my mind to the *kasad* from Damascus who brought it. Please, let me have the letter in my hand.'

Handing over the controversial piece of document to his younger brother, Hassan left Muhammad's shrine to go to a nearby mosque. Hussein approached the messenger from Damascus. Addressing him, he said, '*Kasad*, I feel like kicking you and your scheming masters today. And I would have given a fitting reply to the note which you took the trouble of bringing here if my kind brother had not forbidden me. I would have stamped my foot on every syllable of that document if it were not written in the script used for our holy Koran. But tell your master Yazid on your return to Damascus, how angry his note has made us. And here, hand this over to him as our answer.' Saying that, Hussein tore the letter into tiny shreds and put them in the *kasad*'s hand. 'And don't forget,' he added, 'to thank the Almighty for saving you from our wrath, which, if we had cared to give you the punishment you really deserve, could have made this evening the last evening of your life.'*

Even before his messenger had returned to Damascus from Medina, Yazid had readied his soldiers for war. He was convinced that the people of Medina would be very angry on reading Marwan's note. Uniforms for every rank of the army, weapons, drinking water and food, tents, animals, and carts and porters for carrying supplies were arranged. In fact, Yazid was so sure of Hassan and Hussein's fury that he feared for his *kasad*'s life. He did not really expect him to return alive, and therefore had made an alternative arrangement to find out what happened at Medina. A network of spies was collecting information for him. It was only a matter of days, Yazid knew, for war to begin. On inspecting his army, he was glad to find both his infantry and cavalry at their peak of competence. Boastfully, he announced, 'Who can defeat me and my trained men—the best in Arabia! Leave alone Hassan and Hussein, if their father Ali, the renowned swordsman, rises up from his grave to challenge us, we will defeat him in no time.'

While Yazid was thus praising his own army, his *kasad*, back from Medina, approached him, bearing the torn pieces of Marwan's letter to Hassan and Hussein. At that sight, and on hearing how rudely Hussein had spoken to the envoy, Yazid shook with rage. Trying to control himself, he addressed his army, 'My beloved combatants, my strength and support,

---

* Refusing to sign allegiance to Yazid was not just a show of ego for the two Ali brothers. Accepting Yazid as the caliph would mean accepting his lifestyle too. But Yazid had a self-centred, greedy, unforgiving, and cruel way of using his powers—negating everything that Prophet Muhammad stood for and wished Islam to mean.

my right arm! I have given you many rewards and have doubled your pay as soon as I took charge of this state. I have looked after you well. Today, I need something back from you. I command you to leave for Medina immediately to kill my enemies. Don't be in a hurry to put back your swords in their scabbards and the arrows in their quivers. Fight till the mission is complete. Your suits, fortified with protective layers of strong material, will keep you safe. I declare a reward of a lakh of rupees* for the severed head of Hassan, and I am sure that with a little effort, you can slay his younger brother too. My inner voice tells me that your swords are thirsting for those two brothers' blood.'

Then Yazid turned to Marwan, 'Dear Comrade,' he called him warmly, 'and my childhood companion, today I appoint you the general of my army. Please march to Medina as my representative for this important mission. You know the depth of my sorrow, my disappointment at losing Zainab to that cheat—Hassan. You know how desperate I am to take my revenge. If you wish to make me happy, lead my army to victory. Please guide them well. I exist like a dead man now. The day I hear that Hassan and his brother are dead, I will start living again. Oh! How happy the news will make me! On hearing it, I will throw the doors of my treasury open, and you, my precious Marwan, and each of my other subjects will be allowed to take as much wealth from it as you want. And yet, there is a word that I hate and fear—*if.* The idea of it gives me the shivers sometimes. If…Marwan, if you do

---

* Throughout his novel, Mir uses the term 'rupees', that is, 'taka' in Bengali to indicate Arabic units of money.

not win, I forbid you to return home. In such a case, put up somewhere close to Medina, and by treachery, tact, cunning, money, or force, fulfil at least the task of killing Hassan. It will be splendid to learn that Zainab has become a widow again. Well, Marwan, what more can I tell you? You can comprehend exactly how I feel.'

Marwan responded to his friend's passionate urgings by turning to the soldiers standing in orderly rows ready for action. 'Bravehearts!' he called them, 'You just heard your master. I join him in his message to you. Brothers, hail Emperor Yazid with all the sincerity of your souls. Wish him joy and victory. Then move forward to bring him glory. I, your general, will follow you like a shadow.'

In a chorus, the soldiers shouted, 'Hail Emperor Yazid of Damascus! Victory be to him!' The army band began to beat its drums. The solemn sound filled the air. The inhabitants of the city wondered with trepidation whether there was a sudden cloudburst. The streets darkened with the dust of broken stones and grains of sand as hundreds of soldiers marched ahead, holding aloft their banners.

However, everybody in the locality was not happy with the massive display of aggression. Some even shed tears, thinking about the possible consequences if Yazid, the tyrant, won. Even so, there were many in the crowd who wished Yazid well and approved of his exploit.

Yazid accompanied his troops to the edge of the city. Then, with special commendation to Marwan and Alid, the captain of his army, and earnest words of encouragement, again, to the rest of the soldiers, he bade them farewell.

Chapter XI

The citizens of Medina were quite displeased with Marwan's letter from Damascus. They discussed it amongst themselves and could not decide what torture by the Almighty would suffice to punish such disrespect for Hassan and Hussein. The old and infirm devotees of the two brothers spent many hours every day, praying for their well-being, while the able-bodied adults said, 'When we are living in this city, who can dare to harm Imam Ali's sons? Any scoundrel who attempts to ill-treat them while *we* are in charge of their safety should expect an early entry to-hell to suffer the agony of being forever on fire.' The overexcited teenagers of the city declared, 'If we had somehow managed to capture the *kasad* from Damascus bringing us those abominable words, we would have beaten him till he was half-dead.'

In this manner, the men and the women of Medina cursed Yazid and his messenger again and again for days. Their anger slowly subsided though, when no other irritating communication followed. As time passed, they grew more and more complacent and went about their daily life in peace. But Yazid was not going to leave them alone.

The sun was barely up on a pleasant morning when the citizens living on the outskirts of Medina heard faint drumbeats accompanied by the sound of marching soldiers. The volume of that rumble increased steadily and, by midday, everyone in the city was aware of it. It was a bright day, and Yazid's insignia was clearly visible on the banners that the advancing marchers held.

Abdur Rahman immediately got in touch with Imam Hassan and his brother to apprise them of the situation and to decide on an appropriate course of action.

After a short discussion, the prominent citizens of Medina resolved to declare war on Yazid's army. As soon as the decision was broadcasted, the people of Medina were excited. It would be a jihad (holy war), they knew, to fight against the enemy of Prophet Muhammad's grandsons, whom they loved more than their own selves. Moreover, every drop of blood shed in a holy war would wash away their sins. Death in such a war would be martyrdom, which would ascend them to heaven.

Not only the able-bodied adults, but also the boys and elderly men of Medina dressed themselves in combat gear. More than a thousand people picked up whatever weapon each could set hand upon and briskly advanced towards the enemy.

Shaken by such a move of their opponents, Yazid's army stopped its forward march and prepared to camp where it had already arrived. Finding them halting, the men in Medina too stopped. Taking positions behind trees and rocks, they kept a watch over the enemy and waited for Imam Hassan's further instructions.

Hassan was at Muhammad's tomb, praying there with Abdur Rahman and other members of his family. 'My God Almighty,' he pleaded, 'I am a poor, dull person without even a formal army under my command. My only strength is my faith in You. My belief in You has given me unshakable confidence. It has given me great courage. For Your sake, I consider my enemy as nobody. Not only one Yazid, I can defeat hundreds of Yazids while You are with me. I am going to war with Your name on my lips as my weapon. My saviour, please guide me!'

'Amen,' said Hassan's companions, and then they recited the praises of Prophet Muhammad.

Mounting their horses immediately thereafter, they rode to the main thoroughfare of the city. The common citizens of Medina surrounded them there and, noticing Imam Hassan on his horse, cried, 'Beloved Master, our king, please don't endanger your life while we are alive to fight for you. Allow us to slay your enemies or be slain by them.'

Getting down from his saddle pensively, Hassan addressed the crowd in front of him. 'Brothers,' he said, 'you call me master and king, but, like each one of you, even I am a subject and a servant of the Supreme Lord of this world. No one else has the right to call himself a king. The pious duty of each one of us is to preserve the righteousness of His kingdom. There are sinners who do not obey His laws. One such arrogant sinner is at our door today. He is a real threat for us with his large army and enormous material wealth. But against his worldly power, we have the magnificent power of our faith. We have to protect the sanctity of His kingdom by upholding the glory of His name. My brothers, Yazid, whose soldiers are camping near Medina, our beloved birthplace, had wanted me to pay taxes to him. I refused. This has angered him, who was already full of malice against me for marrying Bibi Zainab. He wants to kill me now not only to make Zainab a widow again, but also to capture the throne of Medina.

'Dear Brothers, God has created a beautiful world and gifted it to us. Should not we, at least, be grateful to Him? We do not understand the purpose of His ways, but living in His universe and watching how it works, we know how great God is. And yet, Yazid has no faith in such an All-Powerful Being. Yazid, the unbeliever, has come to invade Medina today. He wants to usurp our independence and dishonour our religion. Above all, he wants to kill me. But Yazid is our enemy, primarily because he has no respect for God, Prophet Muhammad, or the holy Koran. Should we not fight such an enemy to the very end? We have nothing to fear, for if we win, our beloved Medina will be saved, and if we lose and die, we will become martyrs....'

Hassan had something more to say, but his words had already excited his subjects so strongly that they ran as a herd, shouting their war cry to kill Yazid's men. Hassan had not anticipated that. He wanted to lead his supporters towards the enemy in an orderly manner. It was not possible any more.

Hassan, Hussein, and Abdur Rahman had moved a little way forward when they were confronted with an extraordinary scene—all the women of Medina had come out of their homes with weapons in their hands, determined to join their menfolk in protecting the holy city. Hassan was moved to tears at their dedication. 'Brother!' he called Abdur Rahman, 'Take Hussein along and advance to the battlefield. Our army needs your assistance. I shall join you in a while after speaking to the ladies.'

Approaching the group of women and dismounting his horse, he politely asked them why they were there dressed as if going to a war.

'O, Great Hazrat,' answered the spokesperson of the ladies, 'we are ready to do our bit for our birthplace. We have offered our husbands, brothers, and sons to the cause of protecting Medina and your valuable life. Now we do not want to be left behind. We also wish to be of some use to you in this crisis. Moreover, Sir, when our masters, our male relatives, are ready to sacrifice their lives, what right do we have of enjoying the peaceful security of our homes?'

A second woman said, 'And though it is true that even one drop of blood of our loved ones makes us, the fair sex, shiver in pain, we are quite happy to see an enemy bleed. We are also quite capable of breaking the skulls of wicked men.'

Hassan was amazed. Humbled, he said, 'I salute your patriotism. But, Sisters, while my brothers and I are alive, you don't have to exert in this manner. I entreat you to go and pray for our victory. That's what is desperately needed at this hour. Do not shame me by coming to the battlefield.'

The women obeyed Hassan, but before turning back, they showered their good wishes on him. 'O God, protect Hassan who is dearer to us than our own lives, and the lives of our husbands, brothers, and sons. Please protect the holiness of Medina and the sanctity of Rauza-e-Rasool (Muhammad's sacred tomb). Let the spirit of departed Ali, Hassan's father, give supreme strength to his son's arms, and let the spirit of gracious Fatima, Hassan's mother, keep him away from the pangs of hunger and thirst,' they prayed.

After the ladies had left, Hassan recited a quick hymn of gratitude to God and hurried towards the war zone. It did not take him long to reach its borders.

A terrible din was rising from the region where the citizens of Medina were speedily annihilating their enemy. Hassan paused to make an assessment of the situation. To his horror, he found that his men, in their extreme zeal to win, had forgotten all the rules and norms of warfare. They were killing their opponents at random!

Hassan's nobleness prevented him from joining in such an unruly strife. He continued to remain where he was.

The citizens of Medina had almost wiped out their foes. Some of their own men had also died. Hussein was in action in the centre of the field, his sword flashing like lightning as it struck down Yazid's soldiers one after another, his white horse and his white clothes blotched with the enemy's blood. Dappled in white and red, he looked like a glimmering, unearthly apparition. Some of Yazid's men, observing Hussein's ferocity from afar, turned back and took shelter in the nearby forests and caves.

Hassan watched everything from his vantage point, but his face remained expressionless. Who knows what he was thinking?

Shortly, victory was conclusive for the people of Medina. There was no opponent left to be killed.

One by one, the heroes gathered in a group, Hussein and Abdur Rahman prominent among them. They soon spotted Hassan standing with his horse at a short distance. '*Lahellaha Ellalaha Muhammadar Rusullalaha* (There is no God but Allah, and Muhammad is His messenger)!' They recited spiritedly before rushing to their leader and embracing him even with their blood-soaked bodies. Hassan showered them with blessings and congratulations. Then they entered their city.

Boys, girls, men, and women of all ages were standing in rows, lining the city's main thoroughfare to welcome the victors. Prayers of gratitude to God were on their lips. Flags waved. Cheers were bellowed over and over again. The inhabitants of Medina would have sprinkled heavenly flowers on their heroes if it was possible, but they had to be content with whatever flora their township produced.

After visiting Muhammad's tomb, the battle-weary citizens took leave of Hassan, Hussein, and Abdur Rahman and went home to rejoice with their families.

Silence had descended on the battlefield after the victorious party left, proudly unfurling their banners and shouting with joy. Now the ground lay covered with dead bodies and carcasses—heads of dead men against torsos of horses, lifeless limbs torn from their sockets and strewn about, and other such gory sights.

There were still a few men from the defeated party alive, hiding behind their dead comrades, pretending to be dead. Now, as couples or singles, they rose up and met one another. Yazid's men, who were hiding in caves and behind trees, also came out. Among them were Marwan and Otbe Alid.

The survivors did not waste time in lamenting the massacre of their colleagues except Marwan, who, breathing a deep sigh of distress, said, 'O Alid, who knew that the people of Medina had so much strength and determination! Anyway, what has happened has happened. Let us not exhaust our energy in mourning the dead. Rather, let us decide at once about our next plan of action. Remember how Master Yazid had used the word "if"? He had shivered at the thought of what would happen to us "if" we were defeated. It seems that he was always aware of the possibility of such an outcome. His advice to me in case of our defeat was not in vain, and I shall follow it to the last letter. It would be so humiliating for me to face the people of Damascus after what has happened. Luckily, Honourable Yazid has given me clear instructions of not returning to Damascus without killing Hassan, and I must stay on here for that purpose. One of my good men, please hurry to Damascus with the current news. Don't hide anything from Yazid. Give him the most authentic report of the battle. And tell him that I am alive and ready to carry out his final command. Also, on my behalf, plead him to recruit a fresh army for capturing Medina. I know that he can easily afford to do that. And I reiterate, don't hide anything of this debacle from him.'

A person named Emran soon started for Damascus with Marwan's message.

Days passed. Marwan and Alid stayed at Medina in disguise, living in a secret hideout, while their assistants— a handful of soldiers—accommodated themselves in nearby caves.

Chapter XII

A few things in the world should be uprooted or extinguished entirely without leaving behind the slightest trace of them: a loan of money, a fire, an illness, and an enemy. If left unfinished, they tend to erupt repeatedly in terrifying forms.

Hiding behind his disguise, Marwan in Medina was secretly exploring the city, seeking ways of killing Hassan. In need of an agent who could perform the assassination on his behalf, he spoke to various people of the city guardedly, assessing their attitudes towards Hassan. At last, he met an old woman who, for a large sum of money, might consent to be hired for that ignoble task.

It was two o'clock at night. Marwan had an appointment with the old woman in front of a cave at the edge of the city. He had already collected information about her and her family in detail, including the status of their finances, and had tempted her with a promise of gold coins.

Marwan hurried along to be at the meeting place on time.

The woman I called 'old' was actually not so elderly, though she looked older than her age because of her crinkled skin and greying hair. Her name was Maimuna. She walked towards her destination with a heavy heart, feeling bad about the treacherous act she had decided to do merely for money. Face uncovered, she looked up at the moon and the constellation of *Adam Surat*—the human-shaped cluster of stars—to keep track of the time. She did not wish to be late for the meeting. The stars twinkled above, as if gesturing her to abstain from what she had set herself to do. Even the silence of the night was heaving a faint whisper, 'Don't! Don't!' But Maimuna's greed for riches was too strong to stop her in her tracks, and she moved on. As she came closer to the appointed location on the outskirts of the city, she hastened her steps.

Marwan was waiting at the entrance of the cave, a little anxious as to whether Maimuna would really come to see him. Noticing her approach, he breathed a sigh of relief.

They started their discussion at once. Maimuna was the first to speak. She said, 'From the way you got in touch with me, I've already guessed what you want. Now, let us be crystal clear about how I collect my remuneration. I know you will pay me well when the job is done. But, Sir, I need some advance. The thing you want me to do is not easy and may take a long time to execute. I might have to suspend all my other means of earning to apply myself mentally and physically to this scheme....'

Marwan quickly placed a few gold coins on her palm and said, 'Besides these, one thousand such coins will be yours at the completion of the job.'

Tying the guineas in her handkerchief, Maimuna said, 'Don't worry, Sir. A person who has several wives is always in danger of his life. Azrile, the agent of death, sits next to him.

I just have to tweak that harbinger of evil a little and tell him to hurry up...'

Marwan intervened, 'Madam, I don't understand what you mean. What is the harm if a good man chooses to keep several good wives?'

Maimuna replied, 'The harm arises from the fact that a man can truly love only one woman. Sister wives complicate and endanger the man's life because they are jealous of his principal partner. A married woman is always ready to inflict sorrow on her sister wives. Anyway, I won't divulge to you just yet how I plan to manipulate womanly sentiments to my purpose. I just can't wait to get this job over with and take my reward from you!'

Marwan looked around him and said, 'We are quite isolated here. Nobody is watching us except the moon. Let us, then, make nature our witness as we finalize our deal. As soon as Hassan is exterminated, I shall give you one thousand *mohar*s of gold. And I don't want anyone else to know about our secret pact.'

Maimuna shook her head, 'Oh no, Sir, I cannot agree to that. Somebody has to execute the murder, and I definitely do not intend to be that person. But I promise you that our secret won't spread beyond my selected assassin.'

Marwan had to consent to that. 'Ok, then, bring in a third person into this if you must, but beware of recruiting another.'

'Depend on me, Sir,' said Maimuna, 'and don't take me for an ordinary woman. I am a full-fledged political strategist. My work is no less important than that of a minister of state discussing methods for a war or a truce with his colleagues. In fact, my contribution should be considered more valuable, as I don't require expensive logistics. I work without weapons or soldiers and still can enter a tightly sealed chamber, if required. I can go where no breeze can blow in. If needed, I can touch the stony heart of a hardened soldier and make it melt. Chaste ladies, who do not expose themselves to the sun or to people outside their families, can be found in conversation with me...'

Marwan interrupted impatiently, 'Ok, ok. Enough of that! I have known people who brag a lot, but are quite inadequate when it comes to executing their duties. However, I *do* trust that you will do the needful for me. And now that dawn is about to break, let us take leave of each other. I shall see you at your home whenever necessary or meet you at this place by appointment.' Saying so, Marwan strode towards the town without delay.

Maimuna returned home in a grave mood. It somehow felt bad to have agreed to commit such a heinous crime. However, determined to rise above her weakness, she spoke aloud to herself, 'Who is Hassan to me? Why should I hesitate to kill him? And, after all, I will only be the medium of his death and not the actual murderer. Surely, that cannot generate much sin.'

She decided to have a few hours of sleep before the day's work began, but her slumber was not restful. Soon, in her sleep, she was shouting, 'No, no, no, not me, not me, it is Marwan!'

Shuddering, she woke up. Who knows what she was dreaming? She steadied herself, 'Rubbish! I don't believe in all that,' she told herself. 'Only fools consider that dreams are for real, when, in fact, they are merely delusions of the mind.'

After sitting still on her bed for a while, weighing her thoughts, she left the room.

A little later, Maimuna emerged from her house looking quite different. Covered in a long, black tunic, she walked in slow, graceful steps, her entire posture calm and dignified.

Chapter XIII

Maimuna proceeded to Imam Hassan's abode, where she was a frequent visitor in the ladies' quarters. Though a little scared of Hassan's eldest wife Hasnebanu, she was a bosom friend of Zaida, his second. She had also tried to befriend Zainab whom Hassan had recently married, but in vain. Zainab kept aloof and spoke little.

Those days, Zaida had a lot to share with Maimuna—how Hassan, passionately in love with his new bride, constantly neglected his second wife, who was up till then his favourite. Maimuna sympathized with her and even wept with her.

Zaida welcomed her best friend, 'Come, Sister, haven't seen you for ages! Where had you been?'

'Dear Zaida, I was engaged in something important. And it concerns you and only you.'

'Me!' exclaimed Zaida. 'How?'

'Dearest,' Maimuna began, 'I was so pained by what you told me the other day—the sorrow that your new sister wife Zainab has brought on you—that I decided to do something useful for you rather than just pay frequent social visits to you and shed tears together.'

'Why bother, my beloved friend!' sighed Zaida. 'I know how much you care for me. But my situation is hopeless. Forget what I had told you the other day.'

'It seems that you are now friends with the new bride,' Maimuna retorted sarcastically.

'Not that!' negated Zaida. 'It's only that I have given up altogether. I'm reconciled to whatever happens to our relationship and only wish for an early death for myself.'

Hearing that, Maimuna began to weep. 'Sister Zaida,' she said, 'don't make me miserable by such bleak words. And, darling, I advise you not to give up. With determination, a person can rise above any affliction. Now, listen to me carefully. What I have to tell you might cheer you up.'

'My greatest well-wisher, I am always eager to hear what you have to tell me,' said Zaida, wiping her tears, 'and I am sure that whatever you tell me will be good.'

'But promise me to keep this only to yourself. Let not another soul hear about what I have come to tell you today.'

'I promise,' said Zaida readily, and waited for Maimuna to speak.

Very gently, Maimuna began to narrate her proposal. She took time over it. She slowly described how rich it could make Zaida. Then, at last, she came to the most disturbing part of the scheme.

Zaida shuddered. She was stunned. She kept on staring at Maimuna. How could her best friend even utter such words! 'Never!' she said. 'I can never do that. Don't you know that my husband is everything for me? He is like a piece of my own heart. I'll die before I kill him!'

'Be patient,' urged Maimuna. 'Calm down and think over the matter leisurely. If you want to remove Zainab from her seat of glory and make her suffer, this is the only way you can do it. The two conditions—Hassan being alive and Zainab's happiness—are connected. You cannot keep one and destroy the other. Don't accept your humiliation so meekly. One has to fight for one's self-respect and happiness. What is the point of wasting one's life in grief? Anyway, I must leave you now. Think over the matter with a clear head and if you still feel uncomfortable, we won't pursue it.'

Once Maimuna left, Zaida tried to occupy herself with housework, but could not concentrate on it. So, returning to the privacy of her own room, she took to bed to think. She reflected on each and every word that Maimuna had uttered, trying to fathom their deepest significance. After brooding for a long time, she imagined a weighing scale with two panes. She set her devotion for Hassan on one pane and all her other sentiments on the other, and discovered that her husband's well-being was her fondest desire in life. The scale always dipped on her husband's side.

After a while, she imagined her husband with Zainab, enjoying her company and loving her. At that, her imaginary scale swung rapidly. Next moment, in her mind, her husband was the least preferred by her. The tray of the weighing scale with her ego and her desire to see Zainab forever deprived dipped to the ground level.

Zaida herself was taken aback by that. Quickly, she tried to revert to her former self of a loving, forgiving wife, but in vain. Her husband's life had no meaning for her now.

All that she cared for was the satisfaction of seeing Zainab vanquished and the gold coins that would be hers if she acted on Maimuna's advice. She went on reflecting on the matter for hours, but at last, her decision was made. Curious to meet her new, ruthless self, she stood in front of her mirror, watching the reflection of her face. Then, putting on her black robe and veil, she left the house.

Chapter XIV

In Arabia, women could move about freely in burqas. Even women of aristocratic families could travel long distances on camels or horses, all by themselves. They did not have to be carried in palanquins with bearers attending to them all the time, like it was done in India. It was easy, therefore, for Zaida to visit Maimuna at her residence, which was only a short distance away, without anybody noticing.

In the privacy of an inner room, Zaida uncovered her face and began to chat with her friend. She let Maimuna know how keen she was to kill Imam Hassan.

Maimuna understood that she had Zaida in her power, who was burning with jealousy for Hassan's new bride. Satisfied, she said, 'Good to know that at last you have noticed the advantage of the scheme. Let us then execute it as quickly as possible. Now hold this little box. It contains a potent concoction. Hide it from everybody and use it cleverly. It will fulfil your wish.'

'Dear Maimuna,' said Zaida, taking the tiny box from her friend's hand, 'how strange that I am accepting my own widowhood so willingly just to make Zainab lose her husband!

Anyway, thanks for your advice and guidance. And I beseech that you don't abandon me when I become a widow. With my husband gone, there will be nobody in the world to care for me except you. And yet, I would rather be a widow than Zainab relishing my husband's love.'

Zaida spoke the last few words slowly and softly with a heavy heart. Soon afterwards, she left for home.

At home, on opening the tiny box and perceiving the poison in it, she was gripped with a sudden bout of fear. Her hands trembled, but not for long. Soon, she was feeling as brutal as ever. She remembered every detail of Maimuna's instructions and began considering where she would mix the potion first.

There was a pot of honey near at hand, and she decided to use it at once. Stirring a portion of the deadly substance in the honey, she kept the container with the rest of the lethal powder well hidden.

Hazrat Hassan used to visit Zaida's suite of rooms every day. Husband and wife would then spend an hour or two in pleasant conversation. For the past few days, however, due to his other engagements, Hassan was unable to come to Zaida. But, on the day Zaida was ready with her poison to kill him, Hassan had hurried to her, feeling guilty of his few days' absence. He had expected that his second wife, feeling neglected, would be annoyed with him, but was pleasantly surprised to find her in the best of moods. Welcoming him into her favourite chamber, she washed and wiped his feet and spoke to him gently. Her mild temper and tender words charmed Hassan so much that he immediately decided to spend more time there than he had earlier planned for.

For his refreshment, Zaida brought him a bowl of honey and a tumbler of water. 'This is good honey. It was highly recommended by the seller,' she announced, 'I bought a pot of it exactly eight days ago and waited for you to come and taste it.'

'I know how you like me to have the best of everything, dear Zaida,' said Hassan, lifting the bowl, 'I am overwhelmed by your love. Now, let me have a drink of what you have saved for me for full eight days!'

Hassan took a sip of the honey and, within a minute, its toxin began to act upon his systems. With his mouth dry, his vision distorted, and his belly hurting, he called in panic, 'Zaida, what is happening to me! How strange the honey is!'

Feigning astonishment, Zaida said, 'It is all because of my ill luck! Who could have guessed that the honey was so bad! Let me taste it and see....'

Ignoring his own condition, Hassan shouted, 'No, Zaida, no! I beg you, don't touch that liquid! It is deadly! Don't go near it, Zaida!'

In a while, Hassan was tossing and tumbling on Zaida's bed, begging God to help him. However, he forbade Zaida to inform others in the household about what was happening to him.

Hassan spent the entire night in Zaida's room, and she nursed him with the gentlest of hands. By dawn, his pain had subsided considerably. Perhaps, the Almighty had answered his prayers. Hassan dragged himself to the sacred ground near Prophet Muhammad's tomb to attend the scheduled first prayer meeting of the day.

There, Hassan felt better until he seemed to be almost normal. However, the action of the poison on his vital organs had left permanent damages—damages so deep-seated that even the positive energy of the prayer ground or the spiritual strength of Hassan's personality were not capable of removing them (he lived for only forty days after the first episode of Zaida's poisoning him). Yet, he told nobody about the last night's incident, deciding to keep it to himself for the time being.

Nevertheless, Hassan wished to spend the next night with Zaida again. He wanted to get a clearer picture of what had really gone wrong the night before in her room.

On the night of the poisoning, Maimuna's spies had brought her the news that Hassan had drunk from the tampered honey and was writhing in pain. She was relieved. 'Any time now,' she told herself, 'cries of mourning will be heard coming from the Imam's house and filling the city.' She herself got ready to join the mourners. However, hours passed and the surroundings were as still as ever. When it was daylight, Maimuna could not contain her worry. She proceeded to meet Zaida at her residence.

Hearing of the account, she sighed, 'What now!' This time, her friend Zaida was stronger than her. 'There are other ways and means of attaining our goal,' she said. 'Go, get me some top-quality dates from the market.'

'How will that help?' asked Maimuna.

'I will use them to poison my husband.'

'Do you expect him to enter your bedroom ever again? Don't you think he has got suspicious? I fear that he would even hate to set eyes on you from now on.'

'Trust me,' declared Zaida, 'I can still charm him. I have not lost my beguiling powers yet, and I know that his weakness for me has not fully died.'

Maimuna was pleased to find her friend so determined. 'Let me get you the dates,' she said and left.

Alone in her room, Zaida examined the bowl from which Hassan had drunk. It was almost full, for he had taken only a large sip from it. 'Alas,' thought she, 'if only he had taken a little more....But I have to keep trying till I succeed.'

She divided the dates bought by Maimuna into two portions, each having the same number of fruit. She, then, put a certain mark on each of the dates of the first portion—a mark easily discernible to her eyes, but camouflaged for others. She made a slit on each of the dates of the second portion and pushed a pinch of poison through the slits of every piece. Finally, she placed both the lethal and the good dates randomly on a beautiful serving dish.

Hassan was talking with his newly-wedded third wife, Zainab. He said, 'Last evening, I had been to Zaida's quarters, intending to spend the night there. But, all of a sudden, a bout of stomach ache came upon me. I was so indisposed that I could not utter even one pleasant word to Zaida, who too was shaken at my condition. It would give me pleasure to spend this night, too, with Zaida.'

Good-natured Zainab readily agreed that Hassan should immediately proceed to meet Zaida. She was of the opinion that all the sister wives of a man should be equally rewarded with individual attention from the husband. She wanted everyone to be happy.

Hassan had not fully recovered from the ravages of the previous night's poison. He had a weakened stomach and felt dreadful. Yet, too eager to discover the true nature of the spurious honey, he decided to visit Zaida as soon as possible.

In Zaida's company, in her bedroom, Hassan raised the topic and wanted to have a look at the flawed honey. 'How could I keep something that has tortured you so much? I have thrown it away—container and all,' Zaida said.

Hassan was flattered by such affection. Taking advantage of his pleasant outlook, Zaida quickly brought in the platter of dates and requested him to have some. Hassan was very fond of dates, but the memory of the previous night prevented him from starting to eat at once. Noticing his hesitation, cunning Zaida began to have the fruit herself. Relieved, Hassan put them in his mouth too, one by one. Of them, a few had poison. He had taken about seven of the dates when he started feeling ill. Full of suspicion, he stopped eating the dates. With a heavy heart, he left Zaida's room without even bidding her goodbye.

Hassan trudged to his younger brother Hussein's chambers to spend the rest of the night. He writhed in pain for hours before heaving himself again to Muhammad's tomb. There, he prayed to the Almighty to take pity on him and spare his life. God answered his prayers again, and Hassan recovered from his physical distress considerably. However, he did not reveal his secret to anybody. Nobody else in his kingdom, except him and the few who had conspired against him, knew what had happened.

The Imam had no doubt now that Zaida was trying to kill him. Though he did not disclose it to anybody, he was deeply hurt. 'Why is she doing this to me?' he asked himself. 'Knowingly, I have not harmed her in any way. As my wife, she ought to be one of my closest well-wishers, sharing my happiness and miseries. God knows why she is behaving this way! Is she angry with me because I have married Zainab? But, being a sister wife is not new to her. She is my second wife after Hasnebanu. Moreover, if she is jealous of Zainab, she should be poisoning *her* instead of me. Indeed, it is dubious, and I now feel that there must be a more complex reason behind Zaida's unexpected behaviour. Anyway, there is danger here, and I must leave this house and its inmates at once.

'When the enemy lives far away, it produces a different kind of worry—for one is anxious about when, how, through which route and method, and with whose help he is going to strike. In my case, it is just the opposite. My enemy is too near—indeed as near to me as my own being. For, a wife and a husband are supposed to share one soul, though they have separate bodies. They also share the same hopes, compassions, and affections. How terrible! One such beloved wife of mine is trying to poison me, her fair hands outstretched to take my life! Let me not stay in this cursed place any longer. It is better to retire into a forest and live with wild animals than being here.'

After reflecting for some time, Hassan decided to move to the city of Mosul, not very far from Medina. A group of friends, including his best friend Abbas, accompanied him there.

The people of Mosul were thrilled to have the Imam in their midst. They welcomed him with joyous offerings of gifts. However, Hassan's life was going through a tragic phase, which did not favour his stay in Mosul for long.

Chapter XV

The first few days in Mosul were peaceful for Hassan. However, danger lurked nearby. He had come to Mosul to avoid Zaida, not knowing that other foes, living in other places, were also after his life. When fate is not agreeable, one cannot avoid one's encounters with distress. And, to make matters worse, one often cannot recognize one's adversary until it is too late.

Imam Hassan was out of favour with destiny since he married Zainab and brought her to live under the same roof with Zaida. Zainab was the main source of Hassan's trouble. Zaida hated him because of her—she had ended Zaida's happiness. Zaida's hatred for him had driven him out of his home. And without the protection of his own setup, he had become an easy prey of another foe.

News travelled to and from Medina and Damascus. Not only Yazid, but also the common citizens of Damascus came to know that Imam Hassan was visiting Mosul.

Now, in the city of Damascus lived an old man, blind of an eye, who hated Prophet Muhammad for offering a new religion to his people. He was dead against the practice of the alternative holy order. The fanatic had taken an oath to destroy as many members of Muhammad's family as was possible by him. The news that Hassan was living outside his fortress-like home of Medina cheered the delinquent. Taking with him a sturdy javelin, the blade of which he had smeared with a deadly toxin, he travelled to Mosul.

On making some enquiries in Mosul, he came to know that Imam Hassan and his retinue had put up in the city's mosque. He quickly hid his weapon close to the mosque, but at a place where he could easily approach it. Then he went to the Imam, pretending to be full of remorse. Falling upon Hassan's feet, he wept, 'Master, save me! The devil had entered my mind and, for all these years, did not let me perceive the glory of Muhammad's religion! At last, God has opened my eyes. The other day in a dream, I saw that you are visiting Mosul. In that same dream, somebody told me, "Go to Imam Hassan immediately. Get initiated in the religion he is preaching—the religion that is true. Confess your sins and ask God to forgive you. Promise God that you will stay away from evil deeds hereafter." That wonderful dream has brought me to Mosul. Now I lay myself at your feet, which are as beautiful as lotus flowers. Do as you please with me.'

Kind-hearted, gullible Hassan, moved by his visitor's pathetic story, consoled him as best as he could and said, 'Let me convert you without any more delay.' Then, with a tranquil gaze and a gentle touch of his hand, he indoctrinated the old man into Islam. As was customary, the new 'disciple' recited the stipulated words that marked his acceptance (in

111

that case, treacherously) of the faith before hugging Hassan's feet, feigning gratitude.

Converting someone into Islam is considered a good deed for a Muslim. So, Imam Hassan was deeply pleased that a person who detested the creed for many years had finally embraced it. He also developed a special fondness for his new disciple, as he seemed to be full of genuine repentance for his mistake. That the man was a villain faking loyalty just to avoid suspicion while waiting for his chance to kill him did not cross the large-hearted Imam's mind. It was not that he did not believe in the precautionary measure of not trusting a stranger fully, but often, to fulfil the Almighty's intended goals such men even overlook their own safety.

Ebne Abbas and Hassan were conversing in front of the mosque. Their new acquaintance had gone out on some errand. Abbas revealed what he was thinking, 'I do not trust that fellow—your one-eyed, elderly admirer from Damascus. He seems to be too full of repentance and too keen to become a Muslim all of a sudden. I have a notion that converting into Islam is not his real purpose of coming to Mosul.'

'I do not agree with you,' responded Hassan, 'If he had some other dishonest intent, where was the need for him to change his religion? He could have committed his crime straight away.'

'True,' replied Abbas, 'but it is also possible that he is making a calculated move by pretending to be your disciple in order to carry out his wicked act. It brings him close to you again and again, for example.'

'Brother, I am not convinced by your reasoning,' contradicted Hassan. 'Why suspect a poor, old man of dishonesty? It is natural that the thought of the Day of Judgement often comes to him now that he is old. If he doesn't regret his misdeeds now, when would he do so? Sins committed always have a way of making a person uncomfortable and remorseful—so much so that the doer sometimes confesses his sins, well knowing that his confessions can even be fatal for him. Sin is not something that can be hidden. Opposed to what you think, our new acquaintance appears innocent to me. The journey from Damascus to Mosul, at his age, must have been arduous. Yet, thirsting for the grace of Muhammad's religion, he has travelled the long route.

'Brother, don't fill your mind with suspicions. If you do that, you will see danger everywhere. Fill your mind with good, positive thoughts, and you will find instances of fulfilment, goodness, and devotion around you. If, as I believe, my new disciple is sincere, imagine how deserving he is of heaven! How glorious are his confessions and remorse!'

Instead of responding to Hassan's speech, Abbas tried to change the subject. Exactly at that moment, the old ruffian from Damascus took his position quite close to Hassan, hiding behind a wall of the mosque and examining the blade of his spear. He was satisfied with his weapon. Should he use it during the next prayer meeting when, in the course of his homage to God, Hassan lay prone on the ground? The weapon then would hit his back and penetrate his heart. But no, during prayer time, the ground of the mosque would be too crowded with devotees for the javelin to have a clear path to its target. It would be better, perhaps, to take a chance while Hassan was only with Abbas, even though Abbas was an exceptionally efficient bodyguard.

Soon, the sinner took his aim. Abbas, though, was watchful. His eyes were everywhere. Suddenly, he spotted the culprit throwing his spear pointed at Hassan's back. Catching hold of Hassan's hand, Abbas pulled him hard. 'O, the devil!' he shouted, 'So, this was what you wanted to do?'

The spear missed its target slightly. Instead of his back, it pierced the sole of one of Hassan's feet. His life was saved by Abbas's alert eyes and timely action.

Abbas was then in a dilemma. Should he attend to the injured Imam or should he run after the assailant and catch him? He decided to do the latter and, dashing after the old man, caught him. Abbas dragged him to where the poisoned lance lay near wounded Hassan and, picking it up, was about to stab the culprit on his chest when Hassan implored him to desist. 'Dear Abbas,' pleaded Hassan, 'spare him. Leave the responsibility of judging my attacker on the merciful Almighty. What has happened is over. Let him go.'

'It is my duty to obey your orders,' said Abbas helplessly, releasing his prisoner, 'but remember to never again fully trust a person before knowing him well.'

The blood oozing from Hassan's wound made red streaks on the floor of the mosque, and seemed to curve, forming the words 'never trust a stranger' in Arabic.

The Imam was in great pain. It was difficult for him to speak, but he did not delay in expressing his gratitude to Abbas for saving his life. 'Abbas,' he gasped, 'thank you!

How clever you are and how amazing is your watchfulness! How penetrating is your vision! You look at a person and can make out what is in his mind. I have not met another with such a talent.' Then, reflecting on his own fate, Hassan continued, 'I wonder what the future holds for me. I have done nobody any harm, but still have enemies everywhere— in one city and another. It is a mystery why people want to kill me wherever I go. I had supposed that Zaida alone wanted me to die. I was wrong. There are many others who would be happy to see me gone.'

The Imam's agony increased by the minute. The pain of his wound was compounded by the action of the poison. 'Dear Abbas,' he moaned, 'take me to my grandfather's grave in Medina. And, as long as I live, I won't leave the sacred chamber that holds it. Coming to Mosul was an error of judgement on my part. Such blunders often bring distress to men. Why did it not occur to me before that my grandfather's burial chamber will be the safest place for me to live in? Please arrange for my passage to Medina as quickly as you can. Even if I die of this wound, it would be a joy to fall into eternal sleep at my grandfather's feet. Azrael (the angel of death) will not dare to torture me at that holy place.'*

The citizens of Mosul, saddened at Hassan's condition, agreed that going back to Medina would be the best thing for him under the circumstances.

---

* Islamic tradition generally holds the angel of death Azrael as a good spirit, who helps dying people make a smooth transition from earthly life to afterlife. However, sometimes, because of their almost similar-sounding names, the spirit of death is mistakenly identified as Azael, who is a jinn (demon). This erroneous mix-up often corrupts the perception of Azrael's benevolence. It is possible that Mir Mosharraf Hossain's depiction of Azrael as fearful is due to this error.

Hassan and Ebne Abbas were soon on the road to Medina.

Muhammad's burial chamber is such a sacred place that no jealousy, enmity, or wickedness can survive there. As soon as Hassan reached that site, he smeared his whole body with its auspicious dust. 'My Lord, save me from this affliction,' he prayed. As if God had answered his prayers, the discomfort induced by toxin in his system slowly subsided and then vanished. However, the mere humans that we are, we do not have the power to understand why something happens while some other things do not. The causes of all such mysteries are known only to the merciful Almighty. Though the poison seemed to have lost its potency, Hassan's wound did not heal. On the contrary, its soreness worsened day by day. The infection advanced to such an extent that the Imam could hardly sit up.

Hussein, Imam Hassan's loving younger brother, was worried about the sanctity of Prophet Muhammad's burial chamber. 'It is true, Brother, that you are safe here from further attack,' he broached the subject while visiting his brother one day, 'but aren't you tainting the pristine holiness of this place by your infected, open wound? A wound like yours cannot be clean. So, it is desirable that you come home. Come home to people who love you and will look after you. A mother is the best nurse, and only she can truly understand the pain of a sick child. Unfortunately, we have lost our mother, but we two brothers are of the same womb. So let me try to give you a mother's care. I will spare no effort in nursing you well.'

Hassan was moved. He was also convinced of the importance of maintaining the sacred chamber's purity.

He readily agreed to go home. Supported by Hussein and Abdul Kasem (Hassan's son), he soon moved to the family's living quarters.

Hassan chose not to enter any of his wives' rooms though, but went straight to Hussein's accommodations.

Every member of the household took part in looking after Hassan. However, the Imam had lost some of his tender naiveté. His suspicion of Zaida had instinctively made him wary of people in general and women in particular. From his attitude towards Zaida, it appeared that he disliked her the most. People wondered why. They found out that Hassan had fallen terribly ill on more than one occasion after being in Zaida's chamber. It gave rise to various rumours, though there was nothing concrete enough in any of them to indict Zaida as a criminal.

As the eldest wife, Hasnebanu was in charge of Hassan's diet. 'Please be extra careful in checking his food for spurious matters,' said Hussein to her one day while visiting the sickroom.

'Oh, yes, Brother,' replied Hasnebanu, 'I taste each and every item myself before giving it to him. Whatever wretched things may have happened in the past, no harm can come to him from food or drink now that I am here to serve him.'

'Thank you,' said Hassan, who had heard the conversation lying in his bed, 'thank you so much, dear Hasnebanu. I need all the care you can give to what I eat and drink.'

From those strange words, it appeared to Hussein and Hasnebanu that probably Hassan was aware that somebody was trying to poison him. Did he know who it was?

Hasnebanu was already very careful about Hassan's meals. Now, she stepped up her vigilance. She stored his food where nobody except her could touch it. The piece of new muslin that covered Hassan's pitcher of water was firmly stretched and stuck to the body of the container with stamped seals. To give the Imam a drink of water, the seals had to be broken and afterwards replaced with new ones.

Customarily, anyone could visit a sick person and attend to his or her needs. So, one day, Maimuna came to see Hassan along with Zaida. There were other people in the room. In fact, people were sitting all around the eminent patient. Zaida and Maimuna sat a little away from the bed.

Maimuna was a respected guest in Hassan's household, as people knew her to be on good terms with the late Bibi Fatima and her sons. Nobody was aware, except Zaida, of the deadly feelings she actually had for the family.

On that visit, tears rolled down Maimuna's cheeks on witnessing Hassan on his sickbed. People said, 'Poor woman, how can she not weep at the Imam's condition? She and Bibi Fatima were friends. Maimuna had assisted the Bibi in bringing up Hassan. We have seen her carrying baby Hassan on her hips and shoulders.'

Teary-eyed, Maimuna looked at each one of the visitors around the patient's cot as if to share her sadness with them. But actually, as she turned her eyes around, she furtively made a mental note of each and every item in the room.

Hassan looked at Hasnebanu and gestured that he was thirsty. Rinsing an *abkhora* (covered drinking bowl), Hasnebanu set it near the pitcher of water, broke the seals of the pitcher, and poured water from it into the cup of the *abkhora*. After Hassan had drunk his fill, the pitcher was again covered and sealed. Keeping the water pitcher in its place, Hasnebanu left the room for some other errand.

The ambiance in the infirmary was quiet and grim. But Maimuna felt like speaking. 'I am sure the wretch who wants to harm him has a heart of stone. The dearest child of heavenly Bibi Fatima, the apple of Prophet Muhammad's eye—how can Hassan be tortured so wickedly again and again? This is the work of a pervert, a lowly, inhuman sinner...'

She had much more to add, but Kasem requested her to stop as the patient was getting disturbed.

Chapter XVI

Maimuna and Zaida were together. Zaida was expressing her frustration. 'Dear Maimuna, I find that when God wants to protect somebody, he is beyond destruction. Even poison can get digested in his belly—not once, but several times! I am trying to sink Zainab's ship of happiness by killing my husband. How strange! Previously, my eyes would always seek my handsome master. Now, as I often find him glancing at Zainab with affection, I hate to look at him and want him to die. My hands, once so keen to offer him wholesome food, are giving him poison! My heart used to weep at his slightest illness. Now I weep because he is living. O Maimuna, I am convinced that Hassan will not die and I shall never have any peace of mind!'

'Keep trying,' Maimuna said encouragingly. 'Though you have failed to kill him at your first two or three attempts, don't dither in making a fourth and, if needed, a fifth try. I give you my word that Hassan will not live beyond that.'

Carefully taking out a tiny pouch from a recess of her waistband, Maimuna continued, 'Look what Yazid has sent me after being informed about Hassan's narrow escapes.'

'What is that?' asked Zaida curiously.

'A lethal substance.'

'Again? I am tired of them....'

'In its original form, this substance is of great beauty and value, but when pulverized, a miniscule pinch of it can kill a human being. A few tiny grains of it entering the digestive system can instantly become fatal.'

'Then there must be danger in even touching it.'

'No, dear, it is absolutely harmless till it enters the food canal. You can even safely rub the powder between your fingers. To be exact, it is ground diamond.'

'Powder of diamond? Okay, let me take it.'

Maimuna put the tiny sachet in Zaida's hand. Accepting the dreadful gift, Zaida sighed, 'But, shall I be able to give this to him? His food is strictly inspected for poison. Only Hasnebanu or Zainab is allowed to touch what he eats. Nobody except the two of them can pass him anything spurious.'

'Don't get so disheartened,' retorted Maimuna. 'There are always ways and means of doing things. If I were in your place, I would have done the job easily. Yes, I agree that his food is strictly guarded. But what about his water? You can mix this in his water.'

'Impossible! Haven't you seen how his water is protected? The pitcher is covered and sealed.'

'Yes, the pitcher is covered, but only with a piece of cloth. Tip some of this powder on the cover and dip it in the water.'

Zaida's eyes widened in excitement. 'Yes, that can be done,' she said. 'But, what if somebody notices me doing it?'

'Find an opportunity. Do it when nobody is looking. I advise you not to rush things. Wait till it is quite dark tonight and people have fallen asleep.'

Maimuna did not let her friend go home immediately. While Zaida was resting under her roof, she sent spies to Imam Hassan's residence to find out whether the people there were relaxed enough for Zaida to enter the infirmary and access the patient's water container without suspicion.

However, Zaida was too worked up to be at ease. She left her friend's house early and nervously paced up and down the various wings of Hassan's lodgings. People noticing her agitation thought that it was the normal behaviour of a wife worried about her husband's health. Hasnebanu, who alone could have guessed that something might be amiss on watching Zaida so edgy, was too fatigued to observe what others were doing.

For some time, Hasnebanu had formed a habit of going to Muhammad's *rauza* at midnight to pray for her husband's recovery. On finding her walking towards that sacred sanctuary, Zaida followed her covertly. Then, standing at a distance, she watched her elder sister wife preparing for a long stint at the tomb. At once, she decided to visit the sickroom.

She found Maimuna close by her side. Out of concern for her friend, Maimuna had followed her. 'Do you think this is the right time?' Zaida asked her.

'Yes!' replied Maimuna.

It was the first night of lunar month Rabi-ul-Awal (the third month of Islamic calendar; as Prophet Muhammad's month of birth, this month is holy). The moon had risen and set within a short time. After that, it was pitch-dark.

Zaida proceeded towards her destination with the pouch of diamond dust.

At the entrance of the sickroom, she stood for a minute to check for any alarming sound, however faint, coming from within. Satisfied, she pushed the door a little. She knew that it would be unlocked to let Hasnebanu in when she returned from her prayers. It was ironic that Hasnebanu herself had made it easier for Zaida to approach her victim.

Zaida slipped into the room. A single lamp was glimmering at a corner. Imam Hassan appeared to be in a peaceful slumber, but Zainab looked distressed even in her sleep. She had the Imam's feet hugged at her breast. There were other family members asleep in the room in their respective beds. But except for a steady sound of collective breathing, the chamber was noiseless.

Zaida stood quietly for a few moments to take stock of her surroundings. While looking around, her eyes fell on the pitcher. She swiftly went to it. After looking around once more to make sure that nobody was watching, she was about to untie her sachet, but suddenly stopped. Pensively, she watched her husband's calm face and relaxed body. Then, her eyes fell on Zainab at the Imam's feet and all inhibition vanished. Emptying the whole packet of powder on the cloth covering the pitcher, she vigorously dunked it into the water.

Work done, she hurried to get out of the room as quickly as possible. In her anxiety, however, her foot slightly hit the exit door and there was a faint noise. The Imam was sleeping lightly. He woke up and looked around the room. Everybody was sleeping. He stared at the door for a moment. It was ajar. Did he have a glimpse of Zaida just outside it? Nobody knows.

The Imam was disappointed that his sleep was broken, for he was into a beautiful dream. 'Zainab,' he woke his bride sleeping at his feet, 'please bring me some water to wash my hands and feet so that I may kneel for worship. I dreamt that my grandfather and my parents are waiting eagerly for me to join them. Such an exquisite dream! So let me pray....'

'I'll bring the water in a minute, Sir,' said Zainab, as she left the room to fetch water for his ablution.

In the meantime, Hasnebanu had said her prayers at Muhammad's tomb. With prayer beads in hand, still reciting the name of Allah, she entered the house and came straight to her husband's side. She found him awake and rather excited. 'Dear Hasnebanu, I was waiting to tell you this,' he said fervently, and went on to relate his dream to her.

Hasnebanu missed a heartbeat on hearing that Prophet Muhammad, Fatima, and Ali had called on Hassan when he was asleep. What did it portend? But she had to keep her reflections on hold, as Hassan needed her attention. 'Please, may I have some water to drink?' he asked.

Absent-mindedly, for she was awfully disturbed by her husband's strange dream, Hasnebanu went through the ritual of serving him a draft. She failed to notice that the cloth cover on his pitcher's mouth had been tampered with.

When Hassan had drunk his fill, he found Zainab waiting for him with his pre-prayer cleansing water. Rinsing his hands and feet, he cheerfully sat for worship—his last invocation to God in mortal life.

In a short time, Hassan's insides were burning. 'What is happening to me?' he groaned. 'Hot needles are rustling inside my stomach! This is not Zaida's room. Then why? Is this poison again? What trick is fate playing on me?'

He had never before suffered such acute pain. The agony was at least four times greater than that of his first intake of poison. He called Abdul Kasem near him, 'Dear Son, please ask Uncle Hussein to come here quickly, for I may not live longer.' Several members of the household, as we know, were already in the room. Many others joined them as they heard of Hassan's worsening pain.

Hussein rushed in to be at his elder brother's bedside. 'O, Hussein,' the Imam spoke through his anguish, 'I think this is the end. But don't be sad, for I just had a happy dream. In a heavenly garden, I met our grandfather and our parents. They consoled me lovingly and told me that I shall soon be far away from my worldly enemies. Then, a faint sound broke my sleep. Sitting up on the bed, I drank some water and right after that started blazing in pain....'

Hussein cried furiously, 'So the source of your symptom lies in that pitcher of water? Let me taste the fluid and find out what is mixed in it!' Moving swiftly, he picked up the water pitcher and was about to drink from it. Dying Hassan, forgetting his own affliction, cried out, 'You must not! You must not!'

Then, with great effort, he dragged himself up to the spot, forced the pot from his brother's hands, and smashed it on the floor, water drenching the area.

Caressing his younger brother tenderly, Hassan softly said, 'Let this pain be mine alone.' Then he suddenly asked, 'Has my face turned green?'

Hassan's face had indeed turned green. Looking at it, Hussein began to weep. 'Don't cry, it is all predestined,' the Imam consoled his younger brother. 'Do you know that our grandfather was once commanded by God to visit heaven even before his death? There, he was shown two decorated rooms—one coloured green and the other red. Do you know for whom the rooms were kept vacant and why were they coloured as they were? As explained to our grandfather by Archangel Gabriel and the caretaker of the place, the rooms were meant for us—you and me! Mine was green because I was marked to die of poison, and yours was red predicting a bloody death for you in battle.'

Hussein was too agitated to calm down on that explanation. 'Sir,' he said, 'I have always been an obedient younger brother to you. But, in this case, I cannot remain still even if you want me to. Tell me who has given you poison.'

'Are you thinking of taking a revenge?'

'Yes, I am. Am I so weak and cowardly that I will sit idle while my brother's killer goes free? Tell me whom you suspect. I will kill him or be killed myself.'

'I know who has poisoned me,' announced Hassan faintly, for, by that time, he could hardly speak, 'but I have forgiven that unfortunate being. I do not have any anger, hatred, or envy for that person, though I cannot understand why I was chosen to be killed. Please do not force me to reveal that poor soul's identity. I have asked God to forgive my enemy and have resolved not to climb the stairs of heaven until He grants us that forgiveness. In case you ever come to know who my killer is, promise me that you will forgive that person.'

Out of brotherly love, Hussein said, 'I promise,' and sobbed bitterly.

Abdul Kasem was standing next to Hussein. Taking his son's and his brother's hands and joining them, the Imam said, 'Dear Hussein, please be my son's guardian when I am no more. He is still a bachelor. My fondest wish is that he and Sakina, your gentle daughter, get married.' Then, untying a tiny amulet from his arm, Hassan gave it to Kasem. 'Wear this, Dear Son,' he said, 'and if ever you are caught up in a difficult situation and do not know how to come out of it, read what is written on the reverse side of this talisman and act upon it.'

Hassan closed his eyes and took a few quick gasps of breath. When he opened his eyes, he wanted to be left alone with Zaida for a few minutes. Zaida kneeled beside him as the others left the room.

'My dear wife,' Hassan addressed her softly, 'you have succeeded in killing me. But I forgive you with all my heart because I still love you. I bless you to have a long and happy life.' Zaida remained silent, weeping. Hassan continued, 'I have forgiven you and asked Hussein to do the same if ever he comes to know that you are my assassin. But I wonder if God can forgive you. On my part, I will beg His pardon for you again and again, and I will refuse to enter heaven until He forgives you.'

It was time for the others to return. All were in tears as they stood silently around. Hassan took leave of everyone. He said how grateful he was to Hasnebanu and Zainab for looking after him well. Suddenly, the Imam saw his grandfather waiting for him at the gate of heaven. 'Yes Grandpa, I know that my time has come,' he said and breathed his last.

It was the fiftieth Hijri year—the first of Rabi-ul-Awal.

Chapter XVII

The city of Medina was under a pall of gloom at the great Hassan's death. For the first ten days, each inhabitant remained paralyzed with his or her own grief, unaware of what others were doing. In Hassan's household, Hasnebanu, Zainab, Saharebanu (Hussein's wife), Sakina, and other ladies sat listlessly, shedding incessant tears. Hussein and Abdul Kasem were deeply engaged in prayers to somehow keep the intensity of their grief at bay. Was Zaida mourning her husband's death too? Nobody knew, and nobody except Maimuna was in the mood to care.

Marwan, Yazid's favourite minister, had promptly sent a report to Damascus on the latest development in Medina. He could not carry the message himself to his master, as his work in Medina was not over yet. He continued to reside at the outskirts of the city in disguise.

One late evening, Zaida was in her quarters, lost in her private thoughts. Though she was not mourning for Hassan, she was also not celebrating her good fortune, opting to keep that for later. On Yazid's orders, Marwan had offered her an attractive deal. She had been delaying her acceptance of it for three days. Some complex emotions were holding her back. Were they attachment and love for her marital home, the memory of her late husband's fondness for her, or the desire to relish Zainab's pain of widowhood by staying near her for a while?

Zaida noticed a covered figure approaching. It came to where she sat in the dark. It was Maimuna, her best friend.

The visitor at once raised the topic that was foremost on her mind.

'O Zaida, three days have gone by! It is not sensible to hold back any longer. Make up your mind quickly!'

'Dear girl, you know that you are the only true friend I have now. Tell me honestly, what is your opinion about the offer?'

'Look, people will talk,' began Maimuna. 'In fact, they are already talking, albeit in hushed tones, asking their listeners not to spread the news. It is true that Hussein is too dazed with grief to pay attention to rumours. But, by and by, even he will come to know what you have done. And there will be nobody to plead for you or to protect you here. In such a state of affairs, is it advisable to stay on in this place? Secondly,' continued Maimuna, 'what if Zainab beats you to that coveted position? We know that Yazid has a certain weakness for her. How long would he take to change his mind if Zainab asks his forgiveness?'

'Dear Maimuna, I have already thought of all that. In fact, I had taken my decision to leave this place right at the beginning. Was only taking some time to announce it for some…some personal reasons of mine. Tonight, I am ready.'

'Where is your luggage?'

'I am already dressed for the journey and have nothing to take along.'

Maimuna and Bibi Zaida left the house quietly. Nobody met them. A heart-wrenching sound of bitter weeping coming out of a window was all that bade them goodbye. They recognized the voice. It was Zainab's. 'Weep, woman, weep,' said Zaida, still jealous. 'All this conspiracy was only to make you suffer.'

A short distance away, the two ladies met some soldiers waiting for them with camels. Nobody spoke, but when Maimuna pointed towards Zaida, the soldiers bowed low to her, and then, with great deference and care, helped her first and then Maimuna on to their respective camels. They rode slowly till Marwan, in disguise, joined them and brought them to the cave that was always used as a meeting site by him and Maimuna. There, the three people spent some time in pleasant conversation. Soon, twenty more soldiers added up as bodyguards to Zaida and Maimuna. Marwan stayed back, bidding them good speed. And the ladies' journey to Damascus began.

The inhabitants of Medina soon discovered that Zaida had left the city. There was no doubt in anybody's mind then that it was she who had taken the late Imam's life. 'How terrible!' they exclaimed. 'How could she have the heart to kill the saintly Imam—her own husband! Sinners like her must be rare even in hell!' People even went on to add imaginary flaws to her character. She was now not only a murderess, but also a fallen woman on other counts.

Hussein, shedding tears of anger and frustration, asked God to give him enough mental strength to forgive Zaida. Zaida was out of his reach by then, but even if she were not, Hussein knew that he would have provided for her complete safety to honour his elder brother's wish.

Chapter XVIII

On getting the news of Hassan's demise, Yazid gave away large sums of entertainment money to his officers. A statewise celebration was declared. The ruler insisted that every subject participate in the fun and frolic. Anybody who was unwilling, he announced, would be counted as a traitor to be beheaded or slashed to bleed until death.

A section of Damascus's population was genuinely happy at the elimination of their monarch's most feared enemy, but the rest of its citizens, sad at the good Imam's death, disguised their true feelings and pretended to be joyous. As for himself, Yazid toasted Hassan's death with a relaxed drink of his kingdom's finest liquor, Maal Anab.

Yazid knew that Zaida had accepted his proposal and was on her way to Damascus, accompanied by Maimuna. He was quite keen to meet the woman who had no qualms in poisoning her husband.

In due course of time, Zaida and Maimuna, surrounded by their security guards, arrived in Damascus as state guests. Yazid, however, did not meet them at once. He sent words to his officers that due to some minor indisposition, he would not be able to see the ladies from Medina that day and planned to meet them directly at court the next morning. 'Meanwhile,' he instructed his assistants, 'put them up in the best rooms in my pleasure garden and see to it that they do not lack anything in the way of comfort or honour.'

So, Zaida and Maimuna were given a richly furnished room with maidservants and menservants to attend to them and sentries to protect them from any harm. By and by, it was sunset time and, in a few hours, the two ladies would retire to bed.

Sleep is a great equalizer. A person hit by a tragedy may spend the whole day in mental agony, but during his sleep he forgets his pain. Even someone destined to be hanged at daybreak forgets his distress when he is sleeping. Conversely, people like Zaida and Maimuna, expecting their rewards, cannot experience their joy when they fall asleep.

Yes, Zaida was overwhelmed by her good fortune. Lying in a gold-framed, feather-soft bed, attended by ladies-in-waiting, she was calculating how much more bounty she would receive in the morning. Firstly, there will be her promised share of money—ten thousand gold coins. Then, she will be made the queen. She will thereafter live in comfort and prosperity every day of her life!

Maimuna was resting in a plain bed, a little lower in height than Zaida's. She, too, was counting her blessings. She could have received her reward there in Medina itself. Accompanying Zaida was her own idea—it was to give herself an opportunity for pressing Yazid for more money.

The two friends were soon fast asleep in their respective beds.

Yazid was in an unusual mood that night. He was relaxing all alone with a cup of his favourite drink, a bejewelled decanter in front of him, a silver lamp, its wick burning with scented oil, throwing a mesmerizing light all around.

It is a proven fact that excessive intake of alcohol adversely affects one's personality. However, I swear that if taken in moderation, alcohol improves a person's outlook on life. Yazid had never felt so remorseful before. His eyes held tears as he remembered what a bad son he had been to his father. Scenes flashed before his mind's eye, as he reflected on his past—his first glimpse of beautiful Zainab, his row with his father due to his desire for her, his treacherous invention of a non-existent sister, and making a fool of Abdul Zabbar.

It was quite late when Yazid slept that night. At dawn, he woke up feeling parched. After quenching his thirst, he looked up at the sky. The pole star was gleaming. Yazid could have gone to bed again, for it was too early to start the day, but he decided against it. He was eager for his morning's appearance in the courtroom of his palace. Exciting events were to happen there—decorating and rewarding Zaida, remunerating Maimuna, Zaida's staunch helper….

Yazid bathed and attired himself carefully. Resplendent in his kingly robe, he came to sit on the throne early. His crown was brought to him on a tray and he wore it without delay.

As commanded by Yazid, Zaida and Maimuna had been ushered to the courtroom sometime before the emperor had entered. They sat on the left side of the royal throne—Zaida on a silver seat, Maimuna on a wooden one. The ministers of state as well as prominent citizens of Damascus, formally dressed, flanked the podium of the throne. People who knew Zaida and had heard what she had done were amazed at her presence in the court. They wondered at her ambition and daring, which they presumed had brought her to Damascus.

Yazid commenced the court proceedings by a long speech, 'My honourable subjects, you must have heard that Hassan, my sworn enemy, is dead.

'He was a conceited fellow who loved to look down upon me because my family is not as well connected as his. He had hurt my feelings several times and had tried to usurp my throne. However, his behaviour towards me in itself was not my main concern. For many years, I had been worrying that the administration of Medina was in the hands of an inefficient and bankrupt man—for that is exactly what Hassan was. Therefore, to do the right thing for Medina, I had sent a respectable *kasad* to him, commanding him to accept my overlordship. Hassan had misbehaved with my *kasad* and had sent him back with my letter torn to pieces. As my reply to that insult, I had declared war on him by sending my soldiers to Medina under the leadership of brave Marwan. Unfortunately, a large section of that army, betraying me, had joined Hassan's men, causing a dismal defeat for us. I had no choice left after that but to take recourse to cunning and deceit to remove my enemy from this world.

'Let me introduce my court to the two remarkable ladies who assisted me in succeeding in that difficult task. Bibi Maimuna, on that wooden chair there, was my dependable contact person throughout the proceedings, and Bibi Zaida, on that silver seat, for my sake, had no hesitation in poisoning her husband several times, in the end taking his life with pounded diamond mixed in his drinking water.

'Gentlemen, I had promised Bibi Maimuna one thousand gold coins for her valuable contribution to my cause (as soon as Yazid uttered that, the chief treasurer of the state brought a bagful of money and placed it in front of Maimuna). Now, I fulfil my pledge.'

Yazid continued, 'With Bibi Zaida, my contract was that after she had killed her husband, I would welcome her on my throne with gifts of one thousand gold coins, rich garments, and jewellery.' Immediately, the items mentioned were placed before Zaida.

'Bibi Zaida,' Yazid resumed after a short pause, looking at Zaida and directly speaking to her, 'if you find it to your taste, please come and seat yourself on the left side of my throne.'

Ecstatic with joy, Zaida came and sat on the throne. 'Let our wedding be solemnized later,' thought she, 'I don't mind as I am already a queen!'

Yazid heaved a sigh of relief before he proceeded, 'My promises met in every detail, let me move on to other matters.' He hurried down a few steps from the high platform of his throne, and came closer to and on the same level with his courtiers. Guessing that it would be most appropriate, Zaida too came down the steps and stood next to Yazid.

'My esteemed guests,' Yazid carried on, 'please listen to me carefully. It is true that I will never forget my indebtedness to Bibi Zaida for killing my prime enemy.'

The speaker's expression changed at that point and his countenance became fierce. 'But how could she do that? How dare she kill a man as good and as honest as Hassan? How could she do that to a husband who loved her? I could so easily tempt her with money because she is a fiend in human shape. What guarantee is there that she would not kill me in turn when others allure her with more money? I am the most prominent ruler in this part of the world. Is it not my duty to judge this case of murder fairly and punish the culprit?' Yazid paused, walked about for a short while, and then reverted, 'I have already decided upon the punishment for her. My decision was made last night before I went to bed.' Pulling out his flashing sword, Yazid cried, 'Take that, you, the killer of your husband!' and slashed Zaida in two pieces. Blood spluttered all around, soiling the rich flooring of the courtroom.

'Now, for the other sinner,' said Yazid. 'Let my men bury the lower part of her body in sand and break her head.'

A bugle was sounded to declare the end of the conference. The emperor and his subjects were soon to leave the courtroom.

Chapter XIX

Half of Yazid's project of destroying Imam Ali's sons was satisfactorily completed. The other half was to begin next.

In Medina, Marwan could now give up his secret role of being Zaida and Maimuna's co-conspirator. He was restless to strengthen the military stronghold that he was supervising at a little distance from the city, for he knew that Hussein, the younger son of Ali, could be defeated only through a battle. Yazid was sending him soldiers in batches, but Marwan felt that they were not sufficient. He wanted to meet his master and plead for a larger army. Moreover, he had heard nothing from Damascus after sending Zaida and Maimuna there, and was curious to know what kind of a queen Zaida made.

'Brother Emran,' Marwan confided to one of his assistants, 'I must make a short visit to Damascus. In my absence, please look after our cantonment. You can engage Otbe Alid to collect information from the city as I used to do. He can be a good spy for you. Then, as soon as I come back from the capital with more soldiers, we will seriously engage in our task of eliminating Hussein from this world.'

In Damascus, Marwan was surprised to learn what happened to Zaida and Maimuna. As they were his useful collaborators, he had really wished them to be treated well. However, he did not dwell on the matter for long.

When Marwan proposed to Yazid for more soldiers to fight the people of Medina, the other state chief minister Haman opposed him. In fact, elderly Haman, the trusted officer of the late Muawia, was totally against war with Medina. In a long hearing, Haman and Marwan presented their respective points of views before Yazid.

'Badshah Namdar, I do not wish to displease you,' Haman had begun with his hands joined in supplication and had continued, 'but I think it is unnecessary to start a war immediately. It is true that Hassan had hurt you deeply by marrying Bibi Zainab, but now that he is dead, where is the need to torture his family? It was unfortunate for us that Bibi Zainab had chosen Hassan over you. But it is clear that it was the bibi's fault, not Hassan's, and she has been punished enough already for her wrong choice by becoming a widow again. My lord, please think clearly. Was Hassan really your enemy? Except for unknowingly causing you pain by marrying the woman you loved, he has brought you no harm. He has neither tried to take back the throne of Damascus from you, nor tried to take your life. So, why don't we leave his family alone? Hassan's son, brother, and other close relatives are mourning his death now. Wouldn't it be cruel to attack them at this time? God would not like it. Then again, by the laws of statesmanship, the dependants of a defeated enemy should be welcomed into the victor's family with grace and kindness.

So, my lord, do spare the mourning household of Hassan. Praise the Almighty for your good fortune, but remember that it is His will that makes one happy or sad. Even the wealthiest person of this world can become a beggar if He wills it.'

Marwan could not stand such sermonizing any longer, 'Enough of that!' he stood up and shouted in anger. 'It is clear that our elderly minister is suffering from senility. Otherwise, how can he claim that one of the two brothers from the same parents can be a friend while the other is an enemy? Isn't it obvious that the idea of revenge is burning in the minds and hearts of Hussein and his associates at this point of time? They are waiting for a chance to crush us. We are in a stronger position than them now. If we are smart enough, we should strike them at once before they recover from their weakened state. And what is that mumbo jumbo about God's will and such things? Don't try to mix theology with real-time politics...'

Deciding that the debate had come to a close, Yazid raised his hand to ask Marwan to stop.

'I agree with Marwan,' he declared. Addressing Haman, he said, 'Sorry, Chief Minister. I cannot take your advice. From the very beginning, Marwan has been the architect of my clash with Ali's family. Let him continue with his strategies. Yes, Marwan, I have soldiers here numbering four times more than what we have at our cantonment near Medina. Take as many as you want from them and start the operation immediately. Defeat Hussein. Cut off his head and send it to me here in Damascus before you imprison the other members of his family.'

'It is my duty to obey you,' said Marwan, bowing low.

Chapter XX

Marwan returned to his garrison near Medina with a large contingent of soldiers, but had to postpone his programme of attacking the city immediately. This was because, as he came to know from Alid, Imam Hussein was spending all his days and nights in the sanctum sanctorum of Muhammad's graveyard. Marwan knew that it would be futile to ask Yazid's army to invade the holy place, as the soldiers either out of respect for the Prophet or out of superstition and fear considered the ground around Muhammad's grave inaccessible for any aggression. Yet, Yazid in Damascus was waiting for Hussein's skull to be sent to him before any other token of victory that Marwan could win from his opponents.

'Brother Alid,' Marwan shared his frustration with his trusted junior, 'this is a disappointing situation. We cannot lay our hands on Hussein as long as he is in Muhammad's *rauza*, while Yazid cannot be humoured until we behead Hussein and sent the proof to him. Subduing the city of Medina by force will be useless if we cannot capture Hussein. What is our best way out?'

After a lengthy discussion, the two loyal servants of Yazid hatched a rough plan by which they could flush out Hussein from his sacred sanctuary.

When it was late evening, they arrived at the boundary of the *rauza* in disguise and, holding the railings, waited for Hussein to notice them. Hussein spotted them after finishing a session of prayers and came to meet them. The two colleagues bowed low and pleaded for his attention to a secret message they had to offer him.

'Tell me what you have to say, strangers, but I cannot welcome you inside the boundary fence. No outsiders are allowed in,' said Hussein.

So, standing on either side of the railings, they had their conversation.

'We are Yazid's men in disguise. We have come to warn you of an imminent danger,' said Marwan. 'Our army is going to invade this holy place. May be, it will happen as early as tonight. Please leave the *rauza* at once, as their primary object will be to kill you. We are devotees of Muhammad, though we work for Yazid. Knowing that Yazid has this plan of ending your life, we couldn't keep ourselves from taking this risky step of coming here. We felt that it was our sacred duty to do so.'

The Imam thanked his two visitors profusely and said, 'But, Brothers, I do not fear for my life. I loved Hassan more than myself. When he is no more, where is the need for me to live on?'

'We know that you have no fear of dying, Sir,' said Marwan, 'but if you are gone, who will look after your family?

The children and the women will be chained and taken to Yazid's capital as slaves.'

'Don't worry, friends,' responded Hussein, 'I won't die so soon. My grandfather had predicted where my death will happen. It will happen in a dry, bare plain called Dast-e-Karbala. Unless I go there, I will not die.'

'It is good to hear that nobody can kill you in Medina,' said Marwan, 'but Yazid's forces may capture and humiliate you. That is worse than death for a dignified and holy man like you. Anyway, we cannot delay any longer. We will be missed at our barracks if we do. But out of our love for you, we caution you to be careful.'

After his callers had left, Hussein remained thoughtful for a long time. That an attack was imminent corroborated with the general information circulating in Medina that the concentration of Yazid's soldiers near the city had recently expanded. It was clear that Yazid had some plans of action, though Hussein was sure that no army in the world would have the courage to assault Muhammad's tomb. Invading the city of Medina itself was another matter though, and it seemed that Yazid wanted to do exactly that. Hussein also knew that in that case, the citizens of Medina would fight for him with their last drop of blood. However, he did not have the heart to get them engaged in such a mission even before their mourning period for Hassan was over. Grief makes the human mind numb and forlorn, unsuitable for hope and resolve. Hussein felt that if his men entered a war in such a state of mind, they would fail to show the magnificent display of will to win that they had revealed in their last encounter with the opposition. Moreover, he himself was so distraught by his elder brother's demise that he would hardly be able to cheer them to victory.

Suddenly, a novel idea struck him. What if he himself left Medina for some time? It was apparent that Yazid's prime objective was to subdue him. If he left Medina, perhaps, the city would be spared.

He remembered Abdul Zeyad of Kufa. Hussein liked the fellow and considered him a good friend—the best in all Arabia. Hussein and his family would enjoy spending some time in Kufa if that could be arranged. But, of course, it would be below Hussein's dignity to beg Zeyad for his hospitality. The Imam wondered if there was an alternative, honourable way of visiting Kufa.

Returning to camp and emerging from their disguise, Otbe Alid and Marwan sat analysing the outcome of their meeting with Hussein. The encounter was somewhat disappointing, as the Imam did not show any inclination for leaving his safe haven. The two friends agreed that something more was needed to be done. They thought of a strategy, which they felt was viable if executed with the utmost secrecy and care. Abdul Zeyad and the city of Kufa featured prominently in that plan. Had their spies informed them of Hussein's fondness for the city of Kufa? Who knows? Anyway, Alid advised Marwan that they should begin working on the scheme at once.

Marwan began by collecting writing material and composing a very special letter for Yazid. 'Be very careful,' cautioned Alid. 'Make sure that the note should seem meaningless if any of our enemies intercept it. Our message should be crystal clear only to Yazid.'

Marwan took time over the letter. Then, the most reliable and experienced *kasad* in the cantonment was entrusted to carry it to Damascus. The *kasad* had to learn the content verbally too in case the written version got stolen or lost before reaching its destination.

The first part of the work done, Otbe Alid and Marwan got busy with the other details.

Chapter XXI

After travelling non-stop for days, Marwan's messenger reached Damascus. Yazid left whatever he was doing to meet him. Opening Marwan's letter eagerly, he read every word of it with interest.

'Yes, what Marwan has suggested contains a lot of merit,' thought Yazid.

After some more reflection on the matter, he wrote a missive addressed to Abdul Zeyad of Kufa. Putting his seal on it, he commanded his treasurer to add three lakhs of rupees with it.

'Please be my messenger too,' Yazid applied to Marwan's *kasad*. 'I will reward you well. Hand this letter and the money to Abdul Zeyad and tell him to expect more from me when the task is done. Moreover, for his cooperation to me in this project, I shall declare him a free ruler released from my overlordship.'

'Now,' Yazid said looking at his treasurer, 'ask my chief executive officer to provide a team of armed guards to protect the caravan carrying this consignment.'

Abdul Zeyad of Kufa, like other rulers of the region, had his individual squads of spies. One of them brought him the news that a messenger was coming to him from Yazid with rich gifts. Zeyad was flabbergasted. What good deed had he done to deserve it? But he did not have to wait long in suspense, for the courier from Yazid soon arrived in Kufa. Zeyad welcomed him cordially, put by the money, and received Yazid's letter with trembling fingers. He kissed it and touched it to his forehead before opening it, as getting a letter written by the emperor himself was a great honour in itself.

Chapter XXII

The content of the letter was serious, and it left Zeyad cheerless for a while. To carry out what Yazid had asked of him, Zeyad would have to give up something he valued—friendship. He would have to betray Hussein, whom he considered to be a good, honest guy.

But Zeyad was neither spiritual, nor a high-principled person to give real value to human relationships. Besides, he loved a good, lavish life, and Yazid had promised him that as a reward for his support. Though sleep came late to him that night, when Zeyad woke up in the morning, he was fully ready to assist Yazid in his wicked scheme.

In a meeting with his ministers soon after, Zeyad announced that Prophet Muhammad, appearing in a dream, had bid him to help Hussein ibn Ali, who was wasting his life in the Rauza Mubarak of Medina. 'When I woke up, the apparition had vanished, leaving in my room a heavenly fragrance,' described Zeyad. 'I decided then and there that I will invite Hussein to Kufa. And he must come here not as a guest, but as the rightful occupant of the throne. For, in all humility, I have made up my mind to abdicate my kingship of Kufa on his behalf. So, from now on, gentlemen, Imam Hussein is your master and not I. Consider me as one of Hussein's servants.'

In Medina, Imam Hussein heard the rumour of Zeyad thinking of inviting him to Kufa. 'O, merciful God, let that rumour be true,' he prayed.

Sure enough, within a few days, a *kasad* arrived in the holy city, bearing a letter for Hussein from Zeyad. In the letter, Zeyad had described his magnificent dream of Prophet Muhammad, the Prophet's message, and Zeyad's resolve to abide by it.

The inhabitants of Medina, who loved Hussein passionately, crowded round the messenger, 'O *kasad*, is it true that our Imam will leave us and go away to Kufa?' they asked. When the *kasad* replied in the affirmative, they wailed, 'But we don't want him to go!'

With Zeyad's invitation in hand, Hussein visited Bibi Salema (Hussein's step grandmother; Prophet Muhammad's sixth wife) at her *hozra* (secluded place) to share the news with her. 'Don't go,' said the bibi emphatically. 'It will not benefit you. If the Prophet were alive, I know that he would not have liked you to leave his *rauza*.'

'But, Grandma, unless I am gone from Medina, Yazid will attack the city. And I cannot keep hiding in the *rauza*, when my people are fighting to save it. That will not be fair,' explained Hussein.

'Do whatever you like then,' retorted Bibi Salema angrily.

Hussein's maternal aunt Umme Kulsum was standing nearby. 'Dear Hussein,' she said, 'don't trust the people of

Kufa. Remember how your father was harassed by them?*
Who knows what is on their mind this time!'

'But Zeyad is a good friend of mine. I know him well. And
now that I have decided to go, please do not hold me back.'

The inhabitants of Medina surrounded Hussein and
appealed, 'Sir, you think that leaving the city will prevent war
and bloodshed. But we want Medina as it is—with you as our
leader. We want it as a place where we can practise our own
way of life. If our city is attacked, we will defend it out of our
own will and not because *you* want us to. You do not owe us
anything. Your concern for us should not lead you to take a
hasty decision.'

That the people of Kufa should not be trusted was in
the thoughts of other senior citizens of Medina besides Bibi
Salema. One elderly gentleman among them could convince
Hussein that at least a party of scouts be sent to gauge Zeyad's
real intentions before Hussein started for his adventure.

A courageous associate of Hussein—Moslem II—
immediately volunteered to set out for Kufa. 'If it is a trap
that Zeyad has laid to catch my Imam, let *me* be caught in it
instead of him,' announced Moslem. Soon, Moslem, his two
young sons, and a contingent of one thousand soldiers took
off for Kufa.

---

*   Around 658 CE, Imam Ali and Muawia had resolved some of their differences
by negotiations. However, many of Ali's subjects in Kufa did not like it. Their
battle cry was: 'Only God had the right to decide', by which they meant that
victory or defeat should be finalized in the battlefield—that there should not be
any compromise between the rival parties. These Kufans, known as Kharijites
(seceders), became staunch enemies of Ali and, in 661 CE, they killed him.

Chapter XXIII

Though the reply from Medina to Zeyad's letter stated that Hussein would happily accept his invitation, he did not arrive at Kufa for many weeks.

Zeyad was worried. Had Hussein seen through his treacherous plan? No wonder if he did, for Hussein was likely to possess supernatural powers, considering whose grandson he was, thought Zeyad. 'What now?' He reflected pensively. 'Is there another way of catching Hussein and presenting him to Yazid?'

Fortunately, for Zeyad, and to his great relief, an ambassador from Hussein arrived before long in Kufa with his two minor sons and one thousand combatants. Zeyad was shrewd enough to instantly grasp the reason of the emissary's arrival—it was to check on his real intention behind inviting Hussein to Kufa. Immediately, he took the stance of an indulgent host. 'Welcome, noble Sir,' he greeted Moslem. 'As my great friend Hussein's representative, you are entitled to the best of everything that this kingdom can offer.'

'Thank you, O King!' said Moslem. 'My master Hussein intends to come here. However, as he is taking a long time bidding farewell to the citizens of Medina, he has sent me to reassure you of his coming.'

Flattered by Zeyad's hospitality, Moslem spent many days in lordly comfort in Kufa. He did not have even a shadow of doubt that Zeyad was genuinely devoted to Hussein. Satisfied, he wrote the following letter to his master:

> Respected Hazrat,
>
> I am safe in Kufa. King Zeyad has accepted me with great kindness. I had no occasion to suspect anything untoward so far. Another happy matter—a large number of Kufa's citizens is devoted to you.
>
> I hope this report will help you take a right decision upon your future course of action.
>
> Your humble servant,
> Moslem

Moslem's letter pleased Hussein greatly. He could no longer be held back from visiting Kufa.

Food and water for the journey were collected. Cases of arms were packed, in case the party was attacked on its way. Horses, camels, palanquins, carts, and wagons were ready.

Besides his children, his wife, his late brother's son, and two widows, many ordinary citizens of Medina came forward to accompany him to Kufa.* Within a few days, Hussein's

---

*   Mir writes that sixty thousand people had accompanied Hussein to Kufa. But Imam Hussein was leaving Medina to save its citizens and, as such, would have probably discouraged his followers to risk their lives by joining him. Considering this, I have replaced the number 'sixty thousand' by 'many'.

caravan was on its way. It was not as though the Imam was unaware of the risks. While his party was on transit, Yazid's men could attack it any time. But he had to hazard that. He had to move from Medina to save its independence, its people's lives, and its sanctity.

The route to Kufa was well known. The travellers passed familiar shrubs, rocks, palm trees, and occasional waterholes. After eleven days of northward journey, the Imam breathed a sigh of relief, for he had reached almost at the threshold of Kufa. What could Yazid's commander Marwan do when Zeyad and he, the two friends, joined forces against him?

But God had planned something else. Though the path had been traversed many times before, the caravan missed the right turn to Kufa and moved further north. Ahead lay Karbala, a vast arid plain fringed with a forest on one side—the forest bordering the great Euphrates river flowing majestically towards Persian Gulf.

Unknown to the travellers, every inch of their journey was being watched by spies—some reporting to Yazid in Damascus, the others reporting to Zeyad in Kufa.

As soon as Hussein's caravan overshot the road to Kufa, Zeyad sent the following missive to Yazid:

> To Emperor Yazid, whose goodwill is my only means
> of survival,
> My lord,
> I was able to trick Hussein out of Medina. He was
> coming to Kufa, but has mistakenly moved towards

Karbala. However, Hussein's ambassador Moslem is currently trapped by me in Kufa with his one thousand supporters. I request you to send a troop of soldiers to Karbala to capture Hussein. On their way to Karbala, the soldiers can slaughter Moslem and his men in my kingdom. Once Moslem is gone, we can concentrate totally on finishing Hussein. I suggest that Marwan's assistant Otbe Alid command these operations.

Your humble servant,

Zeyad

A superfast courier, charging a hefty fee, carried the letter to Damascus.

The news made Yazid happy. 'It seems that all my efforts will bear fruit now,' he told his ministers. 'Gentlemen, start for Karbala at once.' After a minute's reflection, he added, 'Be sure to block all approaches to River Furat (Arabic name for Euphrates). Use as many soldiers as you need to guard its bank. Let the enemies not get a single drop of water. Guard the river day and night. As those scoundrels have overshot their planned destination, their water bags and barrels must be empty. Let them die of thirst now. And another thing. I want Hussein beheaded. Whoever brings me his severed head will receive a reward of one lakh rupees in addition to the rich remunerations I have promised to all of my men.'

One of Yazid's trusted aide Simar stood up and shouted, 'It's going to be me! I'll be the one to cut off Hussein's head. My lord, keep one lakh rupees reserved for me.'

'I'll do that,' responded Yazid and, impressed by Simar's enthusiasm, promoted him to a higher post in the army.

My readers, you have patiently accompanied me throughout this long narrative of *Bishad Sindhu* (*Ocean of Melancholy*). Yet, I have tried to keep a distance from you. I have tried my best to keep my emotions from influencing your perceptions of the characters in the story. But when I think of Simar, I cannot hold back any longer. I *must* express my dislike for him, whatever might be the consequence.

What kind of a creature might Simar be to gleefully agree to behead a saint like Hussein? Was he a fiend in human shape? But I am not supposed to guess what a filthy mind he had, nor begin to imagine how he looked. For mine is a historical and scriptural story. I have to be faithful to my sources. I have to pay attention to what my predecessors have written. They have not written much on Simar, though. I could only gather that Simar was fair. He had a broad, hairless chest and his face was harsh and brutish. He had a mouthful of crooked, oversized teeth.

Sending off his army towards Karbala, Yazid hurriedly wrote a note to Marwan, asking him to annihilate Moslem and his brigade of soldiers in Kufa, as per Zeyad's request.

When the messenger with Yazid's command reached Marwan and his chief assistant, they had already moved towards Kufa. In fact, they were following Hussein's caravan all along with their troops, intentionally maintaining a wide distance, but in readiness to pounce upon it whenever Yazid asked them to. They quickly marched towards Kufa and arrived at the city's gate.

Zeyad, wearing a mask of innocence in the presence of his guest, Moslem, pretended to lament his fate, 'I waited for Hussein to join me, but he hasn't come. Now the enemy is at our door. O, Honourable Ambassador from Medina, tell me what should I do?'

'I will be the first to defend your city,' replied Moslem. 'Please allow me and my men to attack our enemy at once. You can follow us as quickly as possible. God willing, we will teach Marwan a lesson.'

Every able-bodied citizen of Medina was ready to fight Yazid's men. So, as soon as Moslem invited his small band of warriors to repulse the invasion of Kufa, they shouted their battle cry and got on their horses.

The first thing that caught their eyes once outside the city gate were countless banners with Yazid's insignia fluttering in the wind. Drums beat with an ever-increasing volume. 'My men!' Moslem called aloud, 'It is a good thing that our Imam has not reached Kufa yet. Let us take the onslaught of this attack upon ourselves and save the kingdom of Zeyad, our loyal friend. His soldiers will join us in no time.'

One thousand soldiers behind Moslem shouted their approval.

As soon as the last of Moslem's men had passed the threshold of his city, Zeyad commanded the gate to be locked from inside. Then he declared, 'My beloved subjects, I have an important announcement to make. Please remember that I am only a humble servant of Emperor Yazid, and I do only what he bids me to. Now, he has asked for my help in subduing his enemy, the rebellious Hussein ibn Ali and his associates.

Over and over again, they have refused to sign their allegiance to the emperor. Moslem is a staunch supporter of Hussein. So, I had secretly asked Lord Yazid to destroy him while he was living in Kufa. Let Moslem and his troop be slaughtered outside the gate. Don't extend any help to them. Consider this as my strictest command.'

Many of the Kufans were shocked and saddened by Zeyad's treachery, for they loved Hussein; but it was too late to do anything.

Moslem, who was a renowned warrior, and his daring men fought bravely with the invaders. But they were vastly outnumbered and, after a while, badly needed reinforcement. With no help coming to them from the city, Moslem looked behind and found the huge gate shut with the road leading to it empty. In an instant, he knew how badly he had been deceived. 'Thank God, it is I and not my Imam who is in Kufa,' he sighed.

Holding the reins of his steed in his mouth and using two swords, one in each hand, he fought on, killing many of his foes; but, by the end of the day, he and his small brigade from Medina was massacred. Moslem's two minor sons, who were inside the city gates, were also brutally killed.*

---

* In his later editions of *Bishad Sindhu*, Mir has added a sixteen-page-long subplot, describing how Moslem's boys die in spite of a few Kufan citizens trying their best to save them. In the present translation, that subplot is not included. Mir's subplots are not well-received by the critics.

Chapter XXIV

Missing the right turn to Kufa, Hussein's caravan went northward ahead. In a while, the horses' hooves began to make cuplike depressions in the ground. Noticing it, Hussein held up his hand and asked his party to stop. He was reflective and grave, for he knew what that phenomenon meant. It meant that the soil on which the horses galloped was vastly different from that of any other place he had visited. Yes, he remembered now; he remembered that his grandfather had predicted it—his horse's hooves would cut the ground when it reached Karbala.

Hussein looked around. There was a wooded area further on the right. But on his left and in front of him, as far as he could see, was desolated ground covered with nothing but sand. The wind howled as if to groan, 'Alas, alas!'

There was no doubt in the Imam's mind that he had reached Dast-e-Karbala—the place where he was destined to die. He consulted his calendar. It was the eighth day of the month of Muharram.

'Brothers,' Hussein called his people, 'no need to travel further. We have missed Kufa and reached Karbala. Now, this is going to be our camping ground. Fortunately, River Furat flows nearby. There will be no dearth of water.'

The Imam's companions were happy for a respite from continuous travelling.

A group of servants were sent to bring wood and another to fetch water while the tents were being pitched. There descended a pleasant picnic mood over the party. But then, the boys who had gone to collect firewood came back bewildered to tell a strange story. 'The trees are bleeding,' they said. 'Look at our axes! They are bloodstained.'

The campers gathered around to inspect the strange sight. 'What does this portend?' some of them asked.

Hussein tried to reveal to his disciples the meaning of the weird manifestation without putting them into panic, 'This only confirms that where we have come is Dast-e-Karbala. Anybody who dies here goes to heaven. But there is no harm in cutting the wood. Don't get scared.'

The servants who had gone to get water, however, brought back a truly distressing report. They recounted how the bank of Euphrates was guarded by thousands of armed military men, determined to cut off Hussein's party from any access to the river. The sentries had said that they were hired by Yazid and would honour his orders even at the cost of their lives. 'We have spared you this time,' they had threatened the servants, 'but from now on, anyone from your party who comes within the range of our arrows will be killed.'

Gloom fell upon the people of Medina. 'My merciful God, teach me how I can comfort my followers,' prayed Hussein.

At that juncture, another bad news reached Hussein's

party. Four strangers who believed in Muhammad's religion and admired Hussein came to him to warn him of the grave danger to his life. They said that Simar and Omar were already in Karbala, waiting for an opportunity to kill him, while Marwan and Otbe Alid, who had been busy in their operation of slaughtering Moslem and his soldiers with the help of deceitful Zeyad, were expected to reach the vicinity any time shortly.

Hussein was grief-stricken on hearing about Moslem's death. 'Another wonderful life gone for my sake,' he lamented with a sigh.

But the Imam had no time for mourning or for reflecting on the treachery of Zeyad. His people, especially the children whom he loved so much, had only one thing on their minds— water. Alas, he had nothing to give them but the advice, 'Quench your thirst by remembering God.'

Somehow, the eighth and the ninth days of Muharram passed. On the morning of the tenth day, Saharebanu came and stood before Hussein with their infant son. 'I do not ask anything from you but a few gulps of water for this tiny boy. My milk has dried and he is dying of dehydration. Why don't you carry him to the riverside and give him a drink?' she suggested.

'It will not work. You heard how heavily the bank is guarded....'

'But you can still try.'

'Yes, that I can do,' said Hussein. 'I have not begged in my life for anything, but today I shall beg for a cup of water for my child from my enemy's servants. Give him to me,' the Imam extended his hands.

He saddled his horse and, taking the infant on his lap, rode to the waterfront.

He reined in his horse, facing the thick line of armed men. The sun was blazing in front of him, and flanking him for miles was the monotony of light brown sand.

Hussein raised his voice above the wailing wind, 'I am Hussein ibn Ali, Prophet Muhammad's grandson. This is my newborn baby. He is dying of dehydration. I beg you, Brothers, please let him have a drink of water. Even a few droplets will do.'

Hussein stopped for a minute. There was no movement in the ranks of the soldiers.

The Imam called again, 'Quenching someone's thirst is a charity in every religion. Whichever faith you belong to, your God will be pleased with you.'

Nobody spoke or moved in answer to his pleadings. Hussein's eyes searched the whole line of enemy warriors from right to left, keenly seeking for a response to his request. While his head was turned to one side, an arrow came whizzing straight from the front and struck the baby's chest, creating a little fountain of blood.

'My God!' cried Hussein, as he turned his horse towards his tents, blood soaking his clothes and dripping down on dry sand, his baby dead. He came straight to Saharebanu. 'Take him back,' said Hussein, 'I have given him a drink of heaven's coolest water.' Saharebanu fainted after looking at the dead boy.

Among the people who had accompanied Hussein from Medina were Abdul Ohab, his mother, and wife. The mother, though elderly, was a brave and proud woman. 'My son,' the lady said to Ohab, 'how can you sit still when our Imam's family is going through such sorrow? Do you practice bodybuilding only to kill wild animals? Have you forgotten that you are also a trained swordsman?'

'No, Mother, you are mistaken,' replied Abdul Ohab, 'I am burning with anger and am about to leave for the riverside to win access to the water. I was only waiting to bid goodbye to my wife.'

'Don't,' said the mother. 'I suggest you see her only when you come back. The longing to take an emotional leave from your beloved indicates your fear of not coming back. It's better to go without taking her leave. She will be waiting here to welcome you when you are victorious.'

'Hope it works, Mother,' said Ohab with a faint smile. 'Anyway, I don't have the spirit to argue with you now.' He mounted his horse and galloped towards the Euphrates.

Standing a little distance away from the line of soldiers, Abdul Ohab shouted, 'Cowards! Champions at killing infants! Lowly insects who have sold their souls for Yazid's money! Aren't you afraid of the Day of Judgement? Don't you panic that God would have to put you low down in eternal hell? Make me a passage to the river or I shall kill you all.'

After a lapse of some minutes, a well-built warrior on a reddish brown mare came forward to talk to him, 'We took some time to check on your identity and found you to be a grossly common guy. Go back, you fool! We have no time to waste on you. Emperor Yazid won't reward us for killing you. Send the Imam instead. We are waiting for a lion, not a jackal like you.'

Provoked by being called a jackal, Ohab took his horse to the main line of the armed men and began plying his sword at random. The soldiers had no option, but to fight Ohab in self-defence.

Unknown to Abdul Ohab, his mother had followed him to the battlefield. Her heart swelled with pride on seeing his son's bravery.

However, after fatally wounding seventy of his opponents, Ohab himself was beheaded. As his severed head rolled on the sands, his mother, shrieking in distress, ran towards it and, picking it up, rode on Ohab's riderless horse. 'Which one of you has done this? Let that sinner have courage enough to confront me,' she called.

The killer, a conceited man, announced, 'It is I,' and stood in front of Ohab's horse. Ohab's mother threw her dead son's head at the killer's brow so hard that his death was instant.

'Catch her, catch her!' roared the armed men and, within minutes, hacked her to death.

Immediately after the tragic incident, Gazi Rahman, another gallant warrior from Medina, insisted that he would confront the enemy. Kissing Hussein's feet, he started for the battleground.

Rahman also killed a large number of rivals, but in the end was martyred. Next came Zaffar, but he too met with a similar fate.

By and by, every one of Hussein's able-bodied friends from Medina sacrificed his life in fighting for an access to the Euphrates. Hundreds of Yazid's soldiers were killed, but hundreds more came to take their place.

Chapter XXV

The sun was at its zenith, sending hot rays down to the desert. It was still the tenth day of Muharram. Friends and relatives of Hussein were in a pathetic condition without water. In that state of physical agony, they had to endure the emotional wound of losing their beloved heroes. Yet, few tears were shed for the deceased, as the living lacked the energy to weep.

'Alas,' sighed Hussein, 'there is no hope for us. Though the sand of Karbala is soaked (with blood), we still do not have a drop of water. I think we are finished....'

Hearing his uncle lament thus, Hassan's son Kasem stood before him with joined hands and said, 'Permit me, Uncle, to fight and defeat our foes.'

'No, Kasem,' said Hussein, 'you are the only son of my brother who is no more. How can I send you on such a dangerous mission? How can I face your mother if, God forbid, something happens to you? No, you stay, let *me* go there and deal with the situation.'

'Uncle, you are the Imam. It is my duty to protect you. Bless me so that I can fulfil my duty.'

Hussein was mute for a few seconds, his eyes closed, thinking hard. Then he said, 'Nephew, I don't know how to respond to your eagerness. Better to see your mother and find out what *she* has to say about this.'

Hasnebanu agreed with Kasem that her son should be the one to face the enemy. 'You owe it to your father as well as to your uncle. You ought to avenge your father's killers. God will take care of you.'

Kasem was pleased. Touching his mother's feet, he left to get ready for the vital encounter.

'Wait, Kasem, wait,' called Hussein, 'before you leave, get married. Get married to Sakina.'

Kasem was startled. Was that the time to wed? But his uncle insisted, 'I had given my word to your father that this union will take place. And it is your duty, too, to honour your late father's last wish.'

Hasnebanu was also of the opinion that the ceremony should take place. She thanked Hussein for remembering her husband's ardent appeal.

Kasem was still hesitant. Should he consult the message on the amulet his father had given him before his death to guide him through such a dilemma? He did that. Turning the amulet on the wrong side, he found the words 'Marry Sakina' written on it.

So, it was settled that the wedding would take place immediately.

Dear readers, by God's grace, you and I have come this far into *Bishad Sindhu* (*Ocean of Melancholy*). I had not expected my pen to run so fast while narrating this story. But now, I pause.

How should I describe a wedding taking place in such a bleak situation? In our minds, the idea of a wedding is connected with happy times, beautiful things, and pleasant fragrances. But in that nuptial scene, the spirit of celebration was missing.

The few drops of tears that fell on Sakina's shoulder from the eyes of her friends substituted for the ritual bathing performed before a marriage. However, her hair was done up afresh and a few more jewelleries were added to what little she was wearing. Thus, the bride was ready to accept her husband.

Sakina and Kasem were deeply fond of each other. Equal in age, the cousins had grown up together, sharing their varied experiences and impressions. Such a beautiful bond had developed between the two that when they came of age, they desired to be wedded partners. There was perfect understanding and mutual respect in their relationship.

An auspicious moment was chosen. With the sound of the enemy's drums in his ears, Hussein gave away his eldest daughter in marriage to his brother's son. Then, raising his hands to God, he earnestly prayed for Kasem's well-being.

Kasem was about to leave for the arena of war when Hasnebanu pressed the newly-weds to spend a few minutes together. She ushered them to a tent and left them there, saying, 'Take your leave from your wife, my son.'

Inside the tent, the two stood silently for a minute, holding each other's hands and looking into each other's eyes. Kasem then spoke softly, 'It doesn't matter that we have no time for romance. Praised be God that He has given us a chance to elevate our fondness for each other into this magnificent relationship.'

'Yes Kasem,' said Sakina. 'How happy I am to be married to the man I love. But I am fully aware of what lies ahead, and I cannot be consoled by noble words. I pray to the Almighty that He may let us meet again, somewhere far, far away from this place—away from thirst and fear.'

Kasem pulled his beloved to his heart in a loving embrace and kissed her again and again. Then, releasing her, he said, 'You are the wife of a brave man and the daughter of another. Let me go and fight for my people. Can't you hear the drumbeats from Marwan's camp challenging me to confront them? How can I delay further?'

'Go, Kasem,' said Sakina, 'God will watch over you.'

Kasem moved towards his horse and soon hastened to the battlefield.

'If anybody among you is bold enough to stand in front of my sword, please come over!' Kasem summoned on reaching the battleground.

Omar had heard about Kasem's exceptional skill in swordsmanship. So, he asked Varjak, the most renowned swordsman among Yazid's soldiers, to engage with Hussein's nephew.

Varjak retorted disdainfully, 'Don't you know that I am a very superior warrior, famous all over the world? People in Thailand, Egypt, and Rome regard me with respect, for they have seen me win battle after battle. It will be below my dignity to fight with Kasem, a mere boy. However, I have four valiant sons who can subdue the lad, if you want them to.'

Omar accepted the compromise; but, one by one, Varjak's four sons were slain. Amazed at Kasem's ability with the sword, Varjak himself came to overpower him, but was killed too.

Kasem waited for a while, but when nobody else came to confront him, he moved directly towards Euphrates, penetrating through the lines of soldiers guarding its bank, on his way slaughtering many of them.

In order to stop Kasem, the top-ranking officers of Yazid's army began to shoot arrows at him from a distance, which hit the boy and made him bleed profusely. Soon, his already dehydrated body was so weak that he could not hold on to the reins of his horse. Sensing that his master was in danger, the well-trained horse quickly found its way back to Hussein's camp.

The campers, Sakina and Hasnebanu among them, ran out of their tents to meet Kasem, who slowly climbed down his mount, his clothes dripping with blood. Looking at Sakina, he said, 'Look how red I am. Now that I am in the proper wedding garment, let me hold you again.'

Sakina hugged her husband tightly, but soon his body was so limp that she had to lay him down, his eyes closed forever. For a few minutes, the bride forgot to be her practical, sensible self. 'Kasem!' she pleaded. 'Open your eyes. Open your eyes and look at your wife. It's been just a while ago that you married me! I had not applied mehendi on my hands during the ceremony. Now I know why you have coloured my palms with blood. Look how pretty they are now....'

Hussein was devastated at Kasem's death. Addressing his brother in heaven, he lamented plaintively, 'Brother, you had left Kasem in my care, but see what happened! And why did you ask me to give Sakina to him in marriage? She has become a widow on her wedding day! Do you have any idea of how much we are suffering here? The gloom of this camp is unbearable. Soon, I will be taking up arms to kill the enemy soldiers. At the least, it will save me from the constant anguish....'

Hussein's teenage son Ali Akbar, hearing his father grieve, thus said, 'Father, you still have four sons left, eager to face the enemy. Allow me to set out for the battleground at once. I understand how desperate the situation is for us without water. Bless me to die bravely fighting, rather than keeping company with sorrowing ladies in our tents.'

Hussein could not deny his young son the privilege of going to battle before him.

Without inviting anybody for a duel, Ali Akbar proceeded straight towards the salaried foot soldiers guarding the river. The boy was extraordinarily handsome with a divine aura about him. When he was right in front of the soldiers, something magical happened. Spellbound by his noble bearing, Yazid's infantry lost all urge to attack him, especially when they remembered that the child was to die of thirst soon. Many of the warriors left their posts and went elsewhere. Akbar was then almost at the water's edge. But luck did not favour him much longer. Zeyad's army from Kufa had reached Karbala a while ago and, marching ahead, they quickly had the boy within the range of their weapons. Akbar, meanwhile, felt faint with thirst and exertion. He decided to go back to camp for refreshment.

'Father, give me some water to drink. Let me regain my strength and I promise to bring you victory. I was almost at the water, Father! Can you believe it?'

'Alas, your father is powerless today,' said Hussein. 'Not a spoonful of water is at my disposal. But, Son, I can give you my saliva if you care for it.'

Akbar agreed to have that. So his father offered him his tongue. Akbar took it in his mouth and sucked hard at it. The moisture, meagre though it was, refreshed the boy. He rode back to the battlefield and began his assault on the opponents. But the senior army officers on Yazid's side resumed their attack on him from afar. A poisoned arrow suddenly struck Akbar and went deep into his chest. Akbar felt dizzy and blacked out. Before he lost consciousness, in his mind's eye, he saw Uncle Hassan waiting for him with a pitcher of cool water. Akbar fell down from his horse and died soon after.

Akbar's two younger brothers Ali Asgar and Abdullah were looking out of their tent when Akbar's horse returned to the camp with its saddle empty. Realizing what must have happened, the two boys, without waiting for anybody's permission, rode their horses to the field of action. After taking the lives of innumerable foes they, too, were martyred. When their two horses returned riderless, the campers knew what it meant.

Hussein had no reason now to hold himself back from encountering the rivals. Nobody was left to be given the honour of dying before him. His youngest living child Zayn-al-Abidin was not only too young to go to war, but would also be his bloodline's only remaining male member after his death. Though the little boy was desperate for action, Hussein restrained him and, with great affection, explained why he must not go. To Hasnebanu he said, 'I leave him in your care. You know how precious he is.'

Kneeling down, Hussein held up his hands in submission to the Almighty and had his long commune with Him, 'I see Your glory everywhere, My Lord, though I do not always understand Your ways. I am sure You have a reason for everything. Make me an instrument of your benevolence....'

After his prayers, Hussein dressed up for the final undertaking of his life. He wore items of armour that he had preserved with great care for years: a helmet inherited from the Prophet himself; a breast plate used by his father Ali; a waistband once belonging to Hazrat Daud Paigambar; and a pair of socks handed down to him by Mahatma Saheb Paigambar.

Next, he took leave of everybody in the camp. With just the slightest bit of cheekiness, he greeted Sakina by saying, 'Going to meet your husband, my daughter!' Holding his wife's hand, he said, 'You must join me wherever I am. I shall wait for you.'

Looking at the teary-eyed throng around him, he advised, 'Stop all aggression after I am gone. Nobody else should volunteer to confront the enemy. No need for further bloodshed. I am sure Yazid will look after you well. And I know that as soon as he gets the news of our tragedy, my half-brother Hanifa will do everything in his power to rescue you. And remember to trust in God always.'

So, mounting his horse Duldul (also known as Zuljanah), he rode off.

Chapter XXVI

A strange temper of awe filled every rank of Yazid's army on seeing Hussein in person approaching them on his white horse. This was the hero to subdue whom such an elaborate and expensive military operation was under way. Though the men belonged to the opposition, many of them had a grudging respect for him. He was the rebel who dared to refuse the oath of allegiance to the tyrant Yazid. Some of the soldiers were physically scared of him too, suspecting that being the Prophet's grandson, he possessed some mysterious powers.

Reaching the arena of confrontation, Hussein observed the etiquette of warfare prevalent in his days by calling out for his opponent, 'O Yazid, I know you are having a good time in Damascus, while your employees are wasting in Karbala. I would have preferred a sword fight with you, but in your absence, I am ready to engage with anybody who would represent you.'

Yazid's senior army officers had a quick discussion before they chose Abdur Rahaman, one of the most eminent warriors of his time, for subduing Hussein. Abdur emerged from the vast mass of armed men facing the Imam and stood before him. 'Sir,' he hailed his rival, 'taking account of your state of dehydration, we don't want to torture you excessively. Please throw a weapon at me to let me assess how much strength is left in you for battle, and I shall send you an appropriate junior of mine to challenge you....'

'That cannot be done,' said Hussein, 'for I belong to a tribe that never throws the first weapon. It is a code of conduct we strictly adhere to. I appreciate your concern, but you are welcome to use your most powerful arms against me.'

Abdur Rahaman did so, but Hussein fought so skilfully that in a short time, Rahaman was killed.

Watching the episode, the decision-makers on Yazid's side resolved not to send any high-ranking officials to engage with Hussein. Instead, they reinforced the riverbank by deploying more foot soldiers there. After all, the main strategy of the battle was to cut off water supply to Hussein. Let him kill as many of the common solders as he could and then die of thirst.

After felling Abdur Rahaman, Hussein waited for a while to battle with another hero, but when nobody else came to fight with him, he rode straight to the waterfront. On his arrival there, a large number of the foot soldiers left their posts and ran away helter-skelter, many of them to the nearby forest. The combatants who tried to stop Hussein from accessing the river were killed in droves by their opponent's sword. It was not long before Hussein found himself standing next to his horse on an empty beach, the clear stream of Euphrates flowing in front of him.

The seniors in Yazid's camp like Abdullah Zeyad, Omar, Simar, and others, together with some regular infantry, were keenly observing every move of Hussein from a distance, ready to make a swift charge on him if needed.

They observed him hurrying to the water's edge, about to have a drink. But how could Hussein quench his thirst when the visions of his people's parched lips crowded his mind? He remembered brave Kasem and his own boys, including the tiny infant still on mother's milk, dying of thirst. He remembered Ali Akbar accepting his father's saliva. He remembered his other followers, all with their parched lips. No, he would not have a drink. Throwing away the water he had scooped into his palms, he came up the sands and walked ahead.

When he paused, he looked around him and seemed to like the place. There, one piece by another, he removed his armour, beginning with the helmet. Next, he removed his clothing except for his long pants. His horse was next to him, trying to gauge what was happening. With his animal instincts, he knew that whatever it was, was something sad.

As if in a trance, Hussein started walking again towards the forest. Abdullah Zeyad and company quickly closed in on him. Hussein looked at them with expressionless eyes. The enemy stalwarts began to shoot arrows at him. One poisoned arrow struck the nape of his neck. He put his hand there and felt blood. It broke his trance. He remembered where he was—it was Karbala, the place where he was destined to die. He looked up towards heaven. Then, swaying in weakness, fatigue, and the effect of poison, he fell on the ground. Was he dead? The group of people surrounding him wondered. But even if he were really dead, Yazid would not believe it until Hussein's head was chopped off from his body and brought to him.

Hussein was dead or nearly so. That was the time to behead him. Simar was unexpectedly generous to his colleagues and said, 'Go, Abdullah Zeyad, go and get Hussein's head. This is your chance to win a lakh of rupees.'

'I have neither the mood nor the courage to do that,' answered Zeyad.

'What about you?' Simar enquired, looking at Otbe Alid.

'Not me,' said Alid emphatically. 'I have caused enough suffering to Hussein in the course of serving Yazid. I wonder if God will ever forgive me. No, I have no stomach for that prize money. You go ahead....'

Now there was nothing to stop Simar from hurrying to where Hussein lay, who was still not quite dead.

My readers, this was Simar of whom I have spoken earlier. He was one of the filthiest persons that the human race has produced. With no ado, he sat squarely on Hussein's chest and tried to hack off his head with an arched sword.

'Let me breathe,' pleaded Hussein. 'I do not have many minutes to live. Cut off my head when I am gone!'

'Why should I listen to you?' questioned Simar. 'What does it matter to me if you are in agony? I don't care that you are Muhammad's grandson. I am not a believer and do not intend to be one. The money I will get for your head is all that I am interested in.'

'Can you take off your shirt?' asked Hussein.

'Why?'

'I want to look at your chest. It is predicted that my killer would have a hairless chest. I want to know if you really are my killer.'

Simar removed his shirt, showing a broad, hairless chest. Hussein closed his eyes.

Enthused by the knowledge that he was the chosen murderer of Hussein, Simar resumed slashing his neck with the scimitar, but the head did not come off.

'My grandfather often used to kiss my throat affectionately,' Hussein spoke through his heavy breathing. 'That is the reason why it is so sturdy. Turn me over, I pray, and you will be able to cut me easily. Force the blade of your weapon at the bleeding wound on my nape and my head would detach.'

'I'll do my work exactly the way I like it. Why should I take your orders?' retorted Simar.

'Give me a quick relief and I will ask God to forgive you for all your sins,' offered Hussein.

Simar did as Hussein had asked him to, and the head got detached from the body.

Though Simar was a hardened criminal, a shiver ran through his heart. He picked up the celebrated visage from the ground and quickly departed from the scene, leaving his bloodied weapon next to his headless victim.

Uddhar Parva

Operation Rescue

Chapter I

Duldul, Hussein's snow-white horse, was agitated to find his master's head in another's possession. Neighing plaintively, he ran after Simar for some distance, but then returned to examine his beheaded owner with his muzzle.

Marwan, who since morning was commanding Yazid's army from a strategic distance, joined his colleagues, Zeyad and his team. The four or five leading men of that outfit took to shooting their arrows at the horse, intending to subdue and capture him. But Duldul was clever enough to find a breach through the darting arrows and reach his deceased master's camp.

The scene at the camp was horrid. Abdul Ohab's headless body lay at the entrance of a tent. Hasnebanu, holding the blood-soaked body of Kasem in her lap, was in shock. Sakina, grieving at her dead husband's feet, lay as still as a corpse.

Duldul added to the heart-rending picture when, entering the premises of the camp, he convulsed violently and fell dead, his wounds oozing innumerable streams of blood.

Following Duldul, Marwan and his colleagues too had arrived at the camp. They entered it, demanding aggressively,

'Where is Zayn-al-Abidin, where is Sakina....', but the tragic state of affairs at their destination sobered them down. Marwan looked at Sakina at Kasem's feet and wondered whether she was alive or dead. He was about to touch her when, sensing instinctively that her chastity was at stake, Sakina sprang up to her feet, eyes wide with fear and apprehension. 'Who are you? Why are you staring at my exposed face?' she called out.

By that time, a small band of petty soldiers from Yazid's army had invaded the venue of the conquered. They were looting whatever came their way. Sakina looked at them and realized the grave danger she was in. Then her eyes caught sight of Duldul's blood-smeared carcass, declaring her father's ultimate defeat.

With sudden animation, Sakina announced, 'I am Kasem's wife and will always be with him. But, Kasem, I will leave you alone for a while to defend my honour. Lend me your sword, Kasem. Lend me your sword quickly!' Sakina hurriedly pulled out Kasem's sword from its loop at his waistband and stabbed herself to death.[*]

The officers from the opposite party were stunned. Marwan instructed his assistants to be kindly, 'The people here are in a delicate state of mind. Be careful in dealing with them. See to it that no more suicides happen.' Marwan also arranged for security for the vanquished against the hooligans.

Next, Marwan addressed the defeated party, which now consisted mostly of women, 'Respected ladies, I am a servant

---

[*]   It is commonly believed, though, that Sakina did not commit suicide in Karbala, but lived for many years and took other husbands. As related in Fatima Mernissi's book *The Veil and the Male Elite*, Sakina spent her life in the service of Islam and humanity.

of Emperor Yazid. At his command, I had organized this battle in Karbala where you have been defeated. All of you are now Yazid's prisoners. However, I promise to behave well with you as long as you are under my care. I promise to give you a safe and comfortable journey from here to Damascus. Now, please tell me if I can offer you anything to eat or drink.'

The adults kept silent, but the children in the camp shouted in a chorus, 'Water! We want water!'

In a short time, cool water fresh from the Euphrates was served to them.

Before long, the party, with every survivor from Hussein's side in chains, started its journey to Damascus.

Chapter II

O, traveller! O, stony-hearted traveller, for what prize are you running so fast? Why is there a human head pierced at the tip of your javelin? What a terrible thing to carry! Stranger, what are you going to do with it?

Now I recognize you, Simar. You are the man who had no qualms in chopping dying Imam Hussein's head off his body. Please, Simar, do halt for a moment to reply to a query of mine. Did you do that only for money? If so, alas, money or wealth is the meanest thing on earth. I have heard that money tries to make enemies out of father and son, husband and wife, brother and sister, the king and his subjects. They say money is responsible for all the world's rivalries and wars. Yet, how enchanting money is to its desirers—the poor as well as the rich, the young as well as the old, the king as well as his subjects. But let me banish the thought of money from my mind before my hatred for it can kill my creative impulse.

Simar ran and ran without break, propelled by the excitement of the reward he would get in Damascus. The money would be enough to cover all his dire needs, and he would be a rich man henceforth. He was pleased that his reward need not be shared with anybody, for he had done that daring job all by himself—it was he alone who had cut off the Imam's head, as desired by Yazid.

Simar had run steadily all night, and from the next morning till evening; but now he paused. He knew that he needed to rest and eat something before commencing his sprint to Yazid's capital.

The locality he was passing through was Yazid's domain. In his uniform as Yazid's soldier, he was sure to get board and lodging with some householder there. Any resident of the colony, moreover, would be in awe to see a human head stuck to his lance and give him a good hospitality out of fear.

Simar looked around and selected a house to stay for the night. Azar, the gentleman of the abode, welcomed him respectfully. Accommodating him in an outer room of his house, he gave Simar a wholesome meal and a comfortable bed. After his guest had eaten and was resting contentedly, Azar politely asked him a question, 'I am just a bit curious, Sir. May I have your name please, and the identity of the human head you have with you?'

'I am Simar, and the head is of dead Imam Hussein,' said Simar dryly, and gave his host a quick gist of how and why it was in his charge. 'I chose your house to spend the night,' he added, 'as I found figures of gods and goddesses displayed on your porch. This means you are an idol-worshipper with no loyalty towards the Muhammadans, my master's enemies. I feel safe here. If you were a disciple of Muhammad, Hussein's grandfather, I would not have accepted your hospitality.'

'I am very glad to know that you are Simar, one of Emperor Yazid's favourite soldiers,' said Azar. 'I am honoured to have you at home. Hope you have a comfortable night. However, I am a little worried about Hussein's head here. Suppose, someone has followed you to this place. He may come into this guest room, which is not so well secured, and steal it quietly away or snatch it from you if you are awake. I feel the thing is too precious for you to be kept in this room. Give it to me. I will hide it in my inner quarters for the night and bring it back to you at daybreak. You can sleep peacefully, knowing that it is in my care.'

To Simar's ears, the suggestion sounded like the kindest words he had heard in ages, for he was an exhausted man who desperately needed a stretch of peaceful sleep.

With Hussein's head in his hands, Azar waited quietly outside the guest room for a while. Then, making sure that Simar was fast asleep, he rushed to where his family lived and revealed to them whose head he had brought in and what Simar planned to do with it.

Every member of the family—Azar, his wife, and their three boys—was heartbroken and mourned Hussein's death. Though the family had not converted to Islam, Hussein was a great hero for them. After some discussions, they decided that they would never let Simar take Imam Hussein's head to Damascus and were ready to hold on to it even at the risk of their own lives. Their wish was to go to the battlefield of Karbala, find Hussein's body, and join the head to it.

'It is true that we belong to a different religion,' said Azar, 'but we know that Prophet Muhammad was a holy man, whose grandson Hussein, himself so saintly, deserves our deepest respects. Humanly feelings do not depend on what faith one has chosen—for all of us belong to the same breed. How cruel Yazid is to want to mutilate the body of his defeated enemy! How can we tolerate this inhuman act? No, we will not give back Hussein's head to Simar.'

As soon as Simar woke up in the morning and washed up, he wore his soldier's uniform and got ready to travel. Looking towards his host's living room, he called, 'Gentleman, please bring me my parcel. I am ready to leave.'

Nobody answered him immediately, but after a while, Azar came to him empty-handed. 'I have an appeal to make to you, Sir,' he said softly. 'You are a civilized man and so is our lord, Yazid. In that case, it is uncouth to maul and then make a proud display of the earthly remains of your enemy. Let only primitive men and wild animals do such things—not us. I beg you, give up the idea of carrying the late Imam's severed head to Damascus.'

'You have given me a meal and a bed for the night. So I spare your life,' said Simar angrily, 'but do you think I have not understood your cunning? You want to grab the prize money of one lakh rupees by taking the treasured head to Yazid. Rascal, get me that head at once!' Simar raised his voice further and continued, 'Don't you know the nature of crime for someone disobeying any of Yazid's soldiers? The crime amounts to treason against the emperor. Go, get me the human head that lies in your living quarters.'

'Calm down, Sir,' said Azar. 'Do you promise me that you would leave the premises as soon as you get a dead man's head?'

'Yes, yes, yes!' yelled Simar.

Azar rushed to his wife and sons. 'He won't leave without a human head. So, kill me quickly with this scimitar and give my head to him. You can later go to Karbala with the Imam's sacred head and try to find his body,' he said.

'No, Father, I cannot let you die like that when I am alive,' said Azar's eldest son. 'I beg you, give me the honour of offering *my* life for the sake of high principles.'

Azar's eldest son's head was brought to Simar, who shouted, 'Are you trying to fool me? Your lust for money has made you mad. It seems that you have killed your own son. Now, get the other head for me fast!'

My pen refuses to write the details of what happened over the next half an hour or so. But, by the end of that period, that insanely high-minded family had lost its three sons. Simar could not stand it any longer. He plunged his javelin straight into his host's heart. Without a moment's pause, he then rushed into the inner rooms of the house. Finding Hussein's head on a golden tray, he picked it up and stuck it on to his weapon again.

The late Azar's widow gave a fight. 'I won't kill you, woman!' shouted Simar, but during his skirmish with her, Hussein's head got unstuck from his lance and dropped on the ground. The widow picked it up, but Simar snatched it from her hands and was soon on his way to Damascus. 'What use is my life now?' sighed the widow, and killed herself with the scimitar she was holding.

Chapter III

Time, indeed, is the greatest of healers. Within a few days of their capture by Yazid's men, the women and children of Hussein's family stopped weeping bitterly. They had calmed down and were reflecting on the future. One bright spot in their condition was that Zayn-al-Abidin was still alive and well. As Hussein's son, he held great promise for his dynasty. The other members of the household would not hesitate to sacrifice their own lives to keep Zayn-al alive. They wondered what kind of treatment Yazid would mete out to Zayn-al.

Deliberating on such matters, the prisoners trudged towards Yazid's capital between rows of soldiers, their swords and spears flashing in the glare of the desert.

As they came closer to the city, sounds of merrymaking reached their ears. They also heard repeated peals of congratulatory exclamations: 'Hail Emperor Yazid! Glory to his throne in Damascus!'

Simar had already reached Damascus with Imam Hussein's head and the news of a grand victory. Since then, Yazid had been celebrating with his comrades.

When the procession from Karbala reached the city, the triumphant soldiers among them were given a splendid welcome and rewards of greater value than they had expected. In fact, Yazid had ordered for a free flow from his treasury to all his subjects.

Hasnebanu, Saharebanu, Zainab, Bibi Fatima (Imam Hussein's little daughter), and Bibi Umme Salma (Prophet Muhammad's sixth wife) entered the assembly hall in Yazid's palace, quietly cursing their fate. 'Bibi Zainab,' Yazid addressed Hussein's widow tauntingly, 'do you see what perseverance can achieve? You had always hated me and had declined to be the queen of Damascus. Look where you are now!'

Burning with rage, Zainab muttered under her breath, 'You, the non-believer! God will know how to punish you.' She drew aside the cloth on her breast just enough to show Yazid a glimpse of the sharpened dagger she was carrying to kill herself if necessary.

Realizing that suicide was on her mind, Yazid refrained from teasing her for the moment. Instead, he turned to Zayn-al-Abidin. 'Dear Saiyadzada, what are you going to do now?' he asked him.

'Ascend the throne of Damascus after killing you,' replied Zayn-al, with the characteristic abandon of the fearless young.

Yazid broke into a hearty laughter. 'Well, well!' he said. 'And how do you intend to do that? Don't you realize that you are my prisoner and that I can cut you up into pieces and feed your meat to the wolves and dogs?'

'You asked me a question and I gave you an answer, that's all,' replied Zayn-al. 'I find that you are bent upon showing off your power and won't stop even if I am polite. So there!'

'I will show you really something good now,' said Yazid and, pretending to be very gentle, called little Fatima near him, 'Come, child, have some juicy dates. They are especially for you.' Yazid pointed to a golden platter covered with a richly embroidered piece of cloth.

'I love dates,' remarked the hungry child, as she came near the fruit offered to her. She lifted the cloth cover, drew back in shock, and began to weep. Instead of a mound of dates, the platter held the dead Imam's head. 'It is my father without his body!' sobbed the child helplessly.

Hussein's other relatives were stunned. 'O Lord,' they began to pray, 'give us the strength to bear this sight. Tell us how we should react to Yazid's cruelty. Give us wisdom and patience to accept Your ways. We submit to Your will as we always do.'

The people in the room had not yet completed their plea to God when the head on the golden tray began to rise all by itself! It was glowing with magnificent rays of light, which joined the light from the sky. Within moments, the shafts of light from the sky picked up Hussein's head and gently carried it beyond this world. Only a gust of breeze with exquisite fragrance was left behind.

The spectators were awestruck. Yazid looked up again and again to check if there was any hidden contraption to pull the head up, but found only empty space above him.

Fear rumbled in his ruthless heart. Was there really somebody up there to set things right?

Chapter IV to
Chapter XXX (Summary)

The dead heroes of Karbala were granted fitting last rites by God, who sent all His celebrated saints from heaven to Karbala to chaperone the martyrs of the battle to His abode. Archangel Gabriel was the first to come down to earth. He was followed by Adam, Moses, Solomon, David, Abraham, Ismail (Ismail is a more important figure in Islamic tradition than his brother Isaac, who is better known in Christianity), Jesus Christ, and many other great spirits, all temporarily taking bodily forms. Towards the end of that celestial procession descended Prophet Muhammad. Murtaza Ali followed him along with his wife Fatima.

The bodies of the dead heroes were sorted out and given glorious burials. Immediately thereafter, the corpses transformed into spirits and reached paradise, accompanied by the team of saints visiting there.

Yazid was not yet the sovereign of Medina, even though he had vanquished Imam Hussein and his people. To win sovereignty, his name had to be recited as the lord of Medina by Imam Hussein's successor Zayn-al-Abidin at the Friday prayers. But Zayn-al obstinately refused to do so.

Yazid was so angry at that, that he would have killed Zayn-al, if Marwan, his devoted assistant, had not advised him to tarry. Marwan felt that slaying Zayn-al might complicate matters for Yazid at a time when a larger challenge was threatening to confront him.

Marwan had, by chance, heard about that particular impending challenge when he was with Zayn-al and Zayn-al's great-grandmother Bibi Salema. Marwan had heard the Bibi describing how she had sent a *kasad* to the city of Hanufa, the capital of a province called Ambaz, with a letter addressed to its ruler, Muhammad Hanafiyyah.

Now, Muhammad Hanafiyyah was Hassan and Hussein's half-brother. Ali ibn Abi Talib had married Hanafiyyah's mother after defeating her in a battle, when she was ruling over Ambaz. Prophet Muhammad had approved of the marriage and had welcomed Hanafiyyah, the child born out of that wedlock, and even lent his own name—Muhammad—to him. The Prophet had predicted that this half-brother would always have great goodwill for Hassan and Hussein and would help them with all his ability in times of crises.

Bibi Salema had sent her *kasad* to Muhammad Hanafiyyah when Hussein's caravan had mistakenly arrived at Karbala, where Yazid's men were waiting to massacre its occupants. In her letter to Hanafiyyah, the Bibi had related how Hassan was murdered and what trouble Hussein had been going through since.

Bibi Salema's *kasad* had reached Ambaz on a day of celebration—the wedding day of Hanafiyyah's daughter. But to be at Hussein's side at his hour of need was more important for Hanafiyyah than indulging in merrymaking. He, therefore, immediately left for Karbala on horseback. On his way, he met a *kasad* from Medina who informed him that Hussein was killed and that Hussein's family was imprisoned and taken to Damascus.

Grieving over his brother's death, Hanafiyyah halted his journey towards Karbala and, camping where he had reached, wondered what to do next. After some reflection, he decided to visit Medina, pay homage to Muhammad at his tomb, and consult with the citizens of that holy city before choosing any course of action.

The people of Medina in the meantime, while mourning the death of their Imam and sorrowing for his family, had decided to attack Damascus. To be effectively led in that manoeuvre, they had even thought of a capable person to be in charge. Yes, everybody in Medina had agreed that Muhammad Hanafiyyah of Ambaz should be trusted with the responsibility.

A *kasad* was sent to Muhammad Hanafiyyah from the citizens of Medina not only to invite him to be their general, but also to appraise him of the danger to his life. For, anticipating that Hanafiyyah would be in Medina soon, Marwan had arranged for a large contingent of Yazid's army to be at the ready to kill him before he reached his destination.

Hanafiyyah readily agreed to command Medina's army. He realized that a war was soon to ensue, but was well aware of the strength of the opponents. So he did not rush to take an initiative. Instead, he sent messages to other rulers of the region who were his brothers to join him in the good work of rescuing Hassan and Hussein's families from Yazid's hold. Within a few days, Gazi Rahman, Mazhab Kakka, Omar Ali, Akkal Ali (Bahram), and others came forward with their forces to join him. Soon, Muhammad Hanafiyyah was commanding a large army.

The war that shortly started was bloody and long-drawn. Among many other brave warriors, Yazid's loyal minister Marwan lost his life in a difficult confrontation. In the confusion that the war created, Zayn-al-Abidin could slip out from his prison cell in disguise. He somehow reached his friends in Hanafiyyah's camp, where he received an ecstatic welcome. He was soon coroneted by his well-wishers not only as the ruler of Medina, but also of Damascus.

On the whole, the outcome of the war was Yazid's defeat. In the last paragraph of Uddhar Parva, we find Yazid on his horse, all alone, being hotly pursued by Muhammad Hanafiyyah.

Yazid Badh Parva

The Slaying of Yazid

Chapter I to
Chapter V (Summary)

Against the joint forces of Muhammad Hanafiyyah, Gazi Rahman, Mazhab Kakka, and others, Yazid's army gradually weakened and ultimately collapsed. It was a bad defeat. Fortunately, soon after Muawia's death, on Marwan's advice, Yazid had built an underground resort, its entrance on the ground above camouflaged by decorative foliage. During the war, members of Yazid's household were shifted to that hidden quarter, giving no chance to the enemy of torturing them.

The citizens of Damascus were divided into two political groups. The devotees of Prophet Muhammad were loyal to Muawia, while the others were loyal to Yazid. Many of the Yazid loyalists left their homes in Damascus, afraid of the new regime. The devotees of Muhammad who had to keep their preference secretly to themselves till then were overjoyed and were celebrating openly.

It was then time for the victorious party to enter the main palace of the city and set young Zayn-al-Abidin on the throne. But where was Muhammad Hanafiyyah, the leader of that operation? Why was he not with his people at their hour of glory?

The party was soon informed by a spy that Hanafiyyah was racing behind Yazid to kill him, both riding their horses on a rocky terrain. Even though Yazid was within the range of Hanafiyyah's weapons, Hanafiyyah did not shoot at him, as killing someone from behind was against his wartime principles. So, the victory ceremony had to be carried out without Hanafiyyah.

Pursued by Muhammad Hanafiyyah, Yazid urged his horse to go faster and faster, his aim being to enter the safety of his secret garden-house as quickly as possible.

Arriving near the camouflaged door, Yazid climbed down from his horse to reach the sanctuary on foot, but Hanafiyyah was immediately at his side about to strike him with his sword. At that moment, an oracle was heard, 'Don't kill him, Hanafiyyah! You are not meant to kill him. There is a chamber behind that door where Yazid is supposed to burn till the end of the world for his sins.' An image flashed in the sky—the image of Imam Hussein. Hanaffiyah closed his eyes in respect.

Yazid went behind the secret door, but his screams could be heard outside, indicating that he was in pain, as predicted. Smoke could be detected at the outlines of the closed door.*

The war had affected Muhammad Hanafiyyah in a strange way. Instead of rejoicing his enemy's total demolition, he was raging with hate for the whole world. He started killing

---

* The source of this legend: Yazid died only three years after the battle of Karbala. How he died is not very clear. Some say that while on a hunting trip, he got separated from his team. Though his horse returned, Yazid could not be found.

people at random, be they friends or foes. The other stalwarts of his party were at a loss as to how to subdue him.

When the unreasonable aggression of Hanafiyyah had gone on for a while, there was another oracle: 'Muhammad Hanafiyyah, you will be punished for your sin—for killing innocent creatures who have done no wrong, for wounding people when war is over. Till doomsday, you and your horse will be imprisoned in a vault of stone!'

Immediately after the oracle, hundreds of boulders fell from a tall hill nearby to trap Hanafiyyah and his horse in a hollow. His friends tried their best to rescue him, but failed.

Epilogue

God's will was done. People could see—as far as was possible for mortals to see—for themselves how fate dispenses its judgement and how much a sinner must pay for his sins. Everyone learnt his lessons from it. The new monarch and his ministers spent their night in the palace of Damascus, reflecting on Yazid's downfall and Muhammad Hanafiyyah's strange end. Some of them were so excited and happy at their victory that they could not sleep.

Omar Ali and Gazi Rahman were so emotionally affected that tears filled their eyes. Although tired to the bone, they kept awake till morning.

The morning call for prayers (azan) made everyone in the palace leave their beds. After their supplication to God, the party assembled in the courtroom where Gazi Rahman expressed his desire to put the altered situation of the domain under a good administrative control. By and by, the new head of state, in his royal robe, took his position on the throne. On Gazi Rahman's advice, the highly experienced, elderly minister Haman was summoned to take charge of the management of the monarchy. He was offered the post of the chief minister.

Kissing the throne, the new chief minister announced, 'This is not a novelty. The throne has only come back to individuals who truly have the right over it. King Yazid has been destroyed because of his own evil deeds and his father's curses. Hot-blooded and hot-tempered, Yazid has acted impulsively and taken crucial moves without deliberations. He has acted against the common will, against the advices of the wise and the learned, and against the aged, experienced officers of his kingdom who have penetrating foresight. No wonder that Yazid has fallen and lost his life. The actions of immature, unthinking, and arrogant young men often have similar results.' Speaking thus, Haman bowed to his monarch and showered him with good wishes. Then, he took his seat before the king and was anointed as the chief administrative officer of the kingdom.

The new king was then ready to visit the holy city of Medina with his family and friends. The king's associates whose home town was Medina were especially thrilled at the prospect of returning there.

Soon, the sovereign, with his victorious army, was marching towards Medina, their glorious banners unfurled and their drums beating proudly. On Gazi Rahman's instructions, a troop of messengers was sent to Medina on horseback to inform its people of the king's imminent arrival. Of course, the people of Medina were already aware of how Damascus had been won by their leaders, and how Yazid, after being defeated, had run away from the battlefield. They had also heard of the strange behaviour of Muhammad Hanafiyyah when the war was over. Such news, though received unofficially from time to time through passers-by, had made them immensely happy. So, they were excitedly waiting to get some official confirmation of what they had heard. Shortly, the royal messengers sent from Damascus reached Medina. Assured by them that the good news they had received was genuine, the citizens of Medina immediately visited Prophet Muhammad's tomb and offered their prayers for their new ruler, Zayn-al-Abidin. Then they engaged themselves in organizing a grand welcome for him.

As days passed, the citizens of Medina became more and more eager to have their new king with them. At last, another team of royal messengers hailed to announce the arrival of the victorious king Zayn-al-Abidin at the outskirts of the city. The messengers informed that after camping for the night near Medina, the party would reach the city at daybreak and enter the residence complex of the township after paying their homage at Muhammad's tomb.

No sooner had the citizens heard the joyful message than their city began to get a festive look. Soon, it glimmered like a heavenly town, worthy of welcoming a great new monarch with his family and his brave, victorious associates.

The tall buildings of the city had banners on their towers, displaying crescent moon and stars on a red background. For many days, blue flags, the symbol of mourning, had expressed the citizens' sorrow over Hassan and Hussein's death. Only on that special day of welcoming Zayn-al-Abidin were those flags replaced by pretty little red, yellow, and multicoloured flags. The houses on either side of the main thoroughfare of the city were decorated with garlands of fresh flowers. With those garlands and the colourful curtains at their windows, the houses looked as if they were situated in heaven.

The wives and daughters of men who had joined the forces of Muhammad Hanafiyyah to kill Yazid were ecstatic. Some of them expressed their joy by putting on festive clothes and jewellery, while the others chose to remain as they were, but stood at the windows or at the front steps of their houses with bouquets or wreathes of flowers in hand. As the sun rose, the city of Medina appeared to be a living entity. Residences of the important officials of the city had visitors in droves— the common citizens attired in their best.

Everybody waited with bathed breath for the arrival of the victorious party. 'Was that the sound of their trumpets and the beats of their kettledrums? Is the ground vibrating with those sounds?' they wondered.

Many citizens of Medina were too excited to fall asleep at night. So, in the morning, as they waited for the new ruler to enter their city, their tired bodies just gave in to slumber. People reclined and fell asleep wherever they were sitting, and slept soundly even without a bed or a pillow. But however peaceful that nap might be, the clamour of their crowded surrounding woke them up in a short while. Up from a deep sleep, for a few moments, they remained disoriented, trying to figure out if they were in such an odd place because of some offence they had committed that deserved punishment. Soon, they were thrilled to recollect that they were there, instead, to cheer their victorious, new monarch. And, they shifted to a more advanced position to get a better view. The enchanting look of the decorated main road and the rows of beautified houses lining it stole away from their bearing any lethargy that might have been left by disturbed sleep. By and by, the men, who were all in new clothes, moved towards the main entrance of the city and stood there, intending to rush out and be with their approaching friends as soon as they were sighted, and usher them in with fanfare.

At last, the victorious party was in view! The infantry, each of its members holding up his banner, was leading the party. Following them were the chief warriors with their arms, marching in order. They entered the city gate with sombre dignity. The army band followed them on their camels, their pipes and drums broadcasting the majesty of the new monarch in a melodious symphony. Next came another batch of soldiers, their faces lit up in joyous smiles, on their bedecked horses. The courageous relatives of the monarch in suits, studded with jewels, were the next to enter the city, mounted on their well-built, sturdy horses. They were surrounded by tall and hefty bodyguards. Next in the procession was a band of horsemen, holding in their hands ornamented banners set on silver and golden poles. Clearly visible on those banners were beautifully embellished images of crescent moon and stars. Following them was a trained camel, carrying a sequinned, white parasol. Under the shade of that parasol rode the noble descendent of Mustafa Muhammad, the new ruler of Mecca and Medina, lord of the Muslim world, and the chief of Islam religion, Zayn-al-Abidin, guarded by a thousand mounted men, their swords unsheathed. The young monarch looked dashing in his soldier's outfit, as he cantered on his horse into the city. The spectators shouted in ecstasy, 'Glory be to our new king Zayn-al-Abidin! Glory to the throne of Medina!' The splendid cries of joy echoed throughout Arabia.

Following the great sovereign, a fleet of camels entered the city, carrying prayer books (*ambai*)* on their backs. The camels were especially attended to by their caretakers.

The grand procession entered the city amid great cheering and elation and proceeded towards the holy *rauza* of Muhammad. The gathering halted there. The heroes, each and every one of them, climbed down from his mount of a camel or a horse. The band stopped playing to observe a period of respectful silence. The banners were lowered in homage to the Prophet. The party led by the great Zayn-al-Abidin went round the tomb seven times to observe the ritual of *tawaf*.**

Soon, the new monarch and his retinue entered the palace of Medina. The warriors joined their families after months of hardships and uncertainty. Thanking God, they entered their homes.

Gazi Rahman and Omar Ali, together with the other leaders of the party, stayed in Medina for several days, serving Zayn-al-Abidin, and then returned to their respective kingdoms. Their feelings were mixed. They were happy at Zayn-al-Abidin and his family's rescue from Yazid's prison, and their final victory over Yazid. But, at the same time, they were sad at Muhammad Hanafiyyah's eternal imprisonment.

---

*   I could not find the meaning of *ambai* even on searching all over the internet and elsewhere. From the context, however, I thought it could be a prayer book. My apologies to my readers if I am wrong.

**   The word *tawaf* means 'going around' in Arabic. In Islam, *tawaf* is a respectful ritual where pilgrims go around a holy place—generally seven anticlockwise turns. It is a significant ritual at hajj.

Translator's Acknowledgements

My tribute to the memory of the novelist Mir Mosharraf Hossain. My indebtedness to Niyogi Books for their kind and encouraging response to my project. High regards for Dr Nirmal Kanti Bhattacharjee, Editorial Director of the company, for his professional aid to the work. A big 'thank you' to Ms Sukanya Sur for editing my manuscript with acumen.

My praise for Sri Samir Shome, my husband, for always being the person I love to look up to.

My gratitude to Sri Dipankar Mitra, my large-hearted friend, for gifting me his own copy of *Bishad Sindhu*. I could not have begun my work without that!

Minakshi di (Debjani Chaliha, the eminent Manipuri dancer), for sending me a special edition of *Bishad Sindhu*, published in Bangladesh. It was a boon for my mission.

Warm greetings to my children and their spouses, my brother Uday, sister-in-law Paromita, and my other relatives and friends for their cheer and encouragement.